The DANGEROUS SEX Chronicles Vol. 1 of 3
Beverly Hills, CA
Copyright © 2017 by Biz-e-Bee Book Group
8549 Wilshire Blvd. #139
Beverly Hills, California
All Rights Reserved
Printed and Bound in the United States of America
Published by:
Biz-e-Bee Book Group
Beverly Hills, California
www.bebpub.com
Cover Design by: Biz-e-Bee Book Group
Edited by: Biz-e-Bee Book Group
Formatting by: Biz-e-Bee Book Group
First Printing, February 2009
10 9 8 7 6 5 4 3 2 1
ISBN# 978-0-9817074-1-9
Library of Congress Cataloging-in-Publication Data
Distributed by:
Milligan Books, Inc.
1425 W. Manchester Ave., Suite C
Los Angeles, California 90047
www.milliganbooks.com
drrosie@aol.com
(323) 750-3592

Publisher's Note

3

"Biz was always destined to do something significant."

~Donnie Williams (Los Angeles)

"I was awarded the nickname "Fly Ty" not just because of my fly & fancy buttons and threads, but also for the way I have with words. Upon hearing stories and exchanging words with Biz, I've learned that he also play with them 26 alphabets. I'm going to give him the "Fly" part of my name... he deserves it. His story is Ty-rrific."

~Tyrone Brown
(Philadelphia)

"Biz has graciously presented an intricate chapter in confidence. I selfishly molded this author into perfection because he undeniably represents the truth in its rare form... its cheapa ta keep it real, Playa!"

~Ja'mone Huguely
(Detroit)

"Biz has superb word usage in 'Keepin' It Playa'. It takes off like Carl Lewis and never breaks stride... lames take two steps back... don't hate the playa... Keepin'it Playa is a must read."

~Durward Perry
(E.Oakland)

I LOVE THIS. Biz really is talented. Can't wait to read more. And once again, he had me completely pulled into the story to where I could see it all going down, from the rendezvous to everything going down when you know who showed up. That shyt was crazy. Made me wanna whoop her ass... LOL.

~C. Payne
(Arizona)

This is the first of a series of books of dangerous sex stories. The structure is different and refreshin'. If it is half as fun readin' it, as it was puttin' it together, then you already know the bizness. If you ain't livin', then you dead. Lean back and breathe easy, I'm finna take you on a ride.

~BIZ

TABLE OF CONTENTS

"There is not a man on the earth that only does good and sins not."

~Ecclesiastes 7:20

"I told her that with these big lips, I'd blow bubbles with her cum juice, and I was serious. Later she told me that that line made her pussy drip. That was only the first line."

~Biz

Suck! Suck! Suck!

"Damn Baby that shit feel so good. My dick is sooo hard!"

Suck! Suck! Suck!

"Your mouth is so soft. I'm about to bust!"

Suck! Suck! Suck!

"Damn! Deep throat it so I can cum straight down your throat."

Suck! Suck! Suck!

"Damn! Where do you learn this kinda shit! Ooh shit!"

Suck! Suck! Suck!

"Damn! You must've had a lot of practice! Uh oh, here it cum!"

Suck! Suck! Suck!

"Go deep! Go deep! Ughhhh! Get it! Ughhh! Oh my God! Oh shit! I love you, No, Wait, I love what you do. Have I ever told you that you tha bizness? Wait. Don't even

9

answer that. I know I haven't, couldn't have. I just met you."

Suck! Suck! Suck!

"Ooh, get it! You got me shaking and shit. Ooh, that's it. Get every last drop. Damn! You must've been powerful thirsty. Oh shit! Hold up! What, you tryna suck my soul out? Hold up, wit yo thirsty ass! Oooh!"

Suck! Suck! Suck!

"My God! You do your thing Babygirl, with your fine ass."

Suck!

That one last suck drained me so much I almost fell asleep on that. But I was outside of Stroker's strip club in Atlanta and I wasn't going out like that. The Biz-e-Bee edition Camaro draws too much attention for that.

"Aight Momma. Time to go back to work. I appreciate you."

She wiped her mouth and opened the car door.

"Oh, I almost forgot. Here you go."

I reached in the backseat and got my book and handed it to her.

"Thank you." She said. "I told you I'd do anything for a copy of this book."

When she got out I watched that fat ass sway side to side as she headed towards the club. All she had on was a g-string and bikini top. Damn! Anyway I burned rubbbber out of the parking lot.

I was down in Atlanta promoting "BE LIKE THAT THAT SOMETIMES" and the next day I stumbled across a convention that had in attendance members of 210 book clubsbs there and most of the black popular writers such as Teri Woods, Terry Mc Millan, Vicky Stringer, Eric Jerome Dickey, Iyanla Vanzant, Mary B. Morrison Kimberly Lawson,

Bern Nadette Stanis (Thelma From Good Times) did you know she wrote a book?) and Carl Weber. I Got to expose "BE LIKE THAT THAT SOMETIMES" to an audience who reads the best. What also happened was that I found out that erotic stories were much loved by the ladies. Now I'm the freak of the week. I mean, I think about sex in my sleep, I think about sex in church, I think about gettin' more sex while I'm gettin' sex and I'm a great story teller so I decided to jump genres from Urban lit to Erotica and this is what I came up with. It's called "Keepin' It Playa".

<u>KEEPIN' IT PLAYA</u>

by

BIZ NOLASTNAME

© 2017

It was about 10 o'clock in the afternoon. I was headed northbound on Western Avenue. The music was pumpin' just like the air conditioner was. The car of the day was an S Class 500 Benz, the color of cranberries. Don't take that the wrong way, I'm not tryin' to draw a picture that I have a fleet of high line cars parked in a ten car garage. No, Me and my boys, we roll, get money, so we all have one or two nice cars that we trade off without qualm. I purchased a new Chevy Silverado truck and new Lincoln Towncar, a Towncar, yeah Executive style cause I like to get driven around. I've always heard it said that if you want to be a king you must act as a king.

I sat at the light with my seat adjusted to a position that would have you think I thought I was at home in my Lazy Boy recliner. I donned some skinny jeans and multi-color sneakers this particular day.

My Prada cologne permeated the I-N-T, that's short for interior. I had visited the barbershop early in the mornin' so I was razor sharp at the edge of the follicles. This is normal, so as normal I'm feelin' myself. It was as if the green light was the spiritual signal for her to enter into my life. She slid up on my passenger side in a black Lexus Coupe. The director's cut was perfect. The frame froze. She captured my materialistic nature. Her hair waved as the air flowed effortlessly through it. She carried a Mediterranean complexion and her skin was as smooth as my butt was when I was six months old. A cutie pie, if indeed that term is ever appropriate for a mature young lady that exuded enough confidence to take on this animal in his domain.

Then like a video she continued on in slow motion.

I bit Eve's apple, however, I prefer to think I let her into my world. I keep my charm easily accessible like my gun, my two weapons of choice to make sure things go how I need them to. I reached for my charm and put it on. This is my charismatic character I'm referrin' to. The expression on my face, the look in my eyes and the words I mouthed convinced her to pullover. I admit she was beautiful but I still gave her the standard two minute or less introduction-switch numbers-I'll holla at yuh later and keep it movin' game. She gave me two numbers with 702 area codes, her condo in Las Vegas and cell phone. Then she gave me a number with a 909 area code, her parent's house in Riverside where she would be stayin' while in town. Before we departed she did tell me that she had plans on goin' to Magic Johnson's T.G.I. Friday's in Ladera that night, which happen to be a Friday night. Friday and Sunday nights at Fridays is the place to be for sports fans and fans of sports fans, that is to say, ballers and boujie women respectively.

About 10 o'clock that evening my pimp walk through the doors via my VIP face was interrupted when I noticed the prettiest acquisition to my list of phone numbers of the day, standin' in line. I stopped to acknowledge her, as well as to selfishly advertise myself for the beautiful, potential, temporary soulmates patiently workin' their way to the door. As usual I'm feelin' myself.

I signaled for her to come join me in my immediate entrance. She obliged. We engaged a bit. Two drinks, a few compliments and several touches later I was satisfied with breakin' the barrier of physical contact. She was added to the very, very potential category.

That was okay with me. They call me "Get Around" cause I keep it movin'. I left.

The next mornin' one of my partners in collaboratin' illegal schemes and indulgin' in the good things the cashflow provides, called me from outside my house. He wanted me to ride with him right quick. I hadn't washed my face or brushed my teeth. My boys got me at their disposal, just like I got them, so I rode with him.

I told him, "I'm not gettin' out of this car."

"Aight Man that's cool, I just want you to tell me what you think." he said.

His name could be initials for Tijuana. It wasn't until we were a mile down the road that I found out that I was in for a ride to another county an hour away. He had found a two year old Benz, with seven thousand miles on it, sittin' on a used car lot for a deal he couldn't pass up and he needed my opinion and eye for detail. He did get the car but the reason I mentioned this was because I told him that before we headed out there, to stop at the swap meet in Inglewood, so I could pick up a fresh white t-shirt, some boxers and socks. I would stop at the cleaners when we got back and get dressed at his house.

I moved in and out of the swap meet at the speed Clark Kent did when he had on his red and blue spandex. But evidently, not fast enough to beat the bootleg CD man from capturin' my partners attention with new and unreleased music. We ended up being stationary for twenty minutes. Twenty minutes which I ducked back into the car trying to be incognito. Twenty minutes I could've spent expeditiously dapper donnin' myself at home before we left. Of that twenty minutes it only took ten for the gorgeous visitor from Sin City to coincidentally, cross my path and do exactly the opposite of what I wanted done, that is acknowledge me and give me plenty of attention.

Damn she was fine. Uncomfortable, I blatantly shied her away. Dejected, she left.

A couple of months passed. I often scrolled past her numbers in my phone when I was in the A's. I always spend a few seconds contemplatin' on callin' but never did. My rationalization was, "I'll call her when I'm in Vegas. It'll be fun. I'll make it up to her."

Me and my boys get around more than Pac when he made the song. Sometimes we'll go to Vegas just to play for half a day. The couple months passed and it seemed like I went everywhere but Vegas. It's nothin' new, I meet breathtakin' types regularly that live right here in the city and neglect to take advantage of opportunity. Hindsight is 20/20. I should've given her my number.

Serendipity was doin' its thang one Sunday. I slid through Magic Johnson's Fridays on my see who's around, down a French Connection and get back in the streets, routine. (Rewind 8 words back. A French Connection is a Playas only drink. One part Grand Marnier, one part Cognac, preferably Remy Martin. It's smooth tastin' and fast actin'.) She was on the patio with another bombshell and two dudes seemingly, enjoyin' the atmosphere. My attention was displaced. I could no longer hear the words of the voluptuous vixen talkin' about her promisin' modelin' career. The object of my fixation excused herself to the ladies room. I ensconced myself. In other words, I posted up near the side of the restroom door and waited like I was in an alley with a ski mask on and she was in a check cashin' place. When she exited the restroom, I made my presence known armed with a smile and a full round of teeth in the clip. My intent was to rob her of any ill feelings she had towards me. She smiled when she saw me. We exchanged pleasantries. Our chit chat lasted longer than I expected it would, knowin' there was a vacant seat on the patio with her name on it. Not to mention a couple of guys that were payin' for champagne and it wasn't the kind you can find in the supermarket. Eventually, her party brought the party inside. The other female shared our air and was introduced as one of two of her best friends. Her name was Nicole.

"Hello Miss Lady, nice to meet you."

"Likewise, Sir."

"May I say that the two of you are lookin' stunnin', as a matter of fact, the most stunnin'."

I felt the piercin' eyes of the two uncomfortable gentlemen. I wanted to tell them not to hate the playa because I was sure they qualified to drink a French Connection or two. Don't hate the game either, because up until a few minutes ago they were playin' it too, and would be again in the next couple, cause they don't call me "Get Around" for nothin'. She told me that she had moved from Vegas and was staying at her parent's house. In mid-sentence she pulled her phone out of her purse and asked me for my number, although, asked may be a bit subtle for the nature of her request. While she was enterin' my information, I was bettin' myself that her date wanted me dead. Very unplaya. I wondered who do I talk to about a revocation hearin' or givin' this dude a fine for playin' the game without a permit, that's worse than drivin' with no license.

The next day she called and we made arrange-ments to hook up. I met her at her girlfriend's house, coincidentally, on Western Avenue. The same street I first witnessed her beauty, just a few miles down. Maybe that's where she was comin' from when I met her. I took her to a nice low key club in Hollywood but not before we stopped at a liquor store to get a bottle of The Club Long Island Iced Tea. Her beverage of choice, I wasn't mad at that. We finished the drink as we sat in the car parked in front of the club and people-watched from behind tinted windows. If that night had been about partyin' with a crowd of people, this club would have been a bad choice because when we walked in we noticed that there were more people outside than there were inside and there weren't that many people outside. The lack of people wasn't even a factor though, because our chemistry was of the sort that created the universe. She knew nothin' but me. I was the object of her desire. She gave me so much attention that I was feelin' exceptionally sexy. We built up a sweat on the dance floor. I peeled up out of my shirt and went Petey Pablo on 'em, swangin' it above my head like a helicopter. What happened next was a first time for me to experience, witness or even hear about. She dropped it low like girls do, then the next thing I know, she had my dick in her mouth and it was growin' like the metamorphosis from David Banner to the Incredible Hulk, without the green skin. I looked around and of course everybody in the club was lookin'.

OH MY GOD! WHO'S THE MAN?
ME THAT'S WHO!!!!!

My state of euphoria and elation was incomparable to any thus far. The spontaneity combined with the ambiance in the club and the newness of our relationship made this night un-re-occurable. She took me to the point of no return. I needed to do more than I was willin' to on that dance floor. I scanned the environment for a dark corner. My eyes landed on a staircase and followed them up. It was dark up there. My guess was that it was a VIP lounge but there weren't enough guests to warrant even turnin' on the lights. There was nothin' and no one at the base of the staircase to impede our access to take things to the next level in more ways than one. My guess of what the space was designed to accommodate was accurate. The interior designer was liberal. Although cozy with several fluffy couches and a coffee table to simulate the ambience of being in a comfortable livin' room, it was spacious to the effect that it hovered over half of the dance floor, with a ledge allowin' you to see down to the other half and DJ station. On the far left in the darkness was a maroon colored couch, positioned perfect for our perverted propensity to be promiscuous.

There were only two individuals up there, two that were soon to become one. I sat down and within seconds had a déjà vu of her pretty face, seductively, going back and forth on the jewel that I treasured more than the diamonds in my ear.

If I didn't know better I'd say that the DJ was in on it, because at the same time I realized that she was takin' me all in her mouth without gaggin', I also noticed that he was playin' Keith Sweat's classic "How deep is your love." I threw my head back and indulged in the guilty pleasure. Her tongue massaged the lower dimensions of my shaft while her lips tickled the rest of it. She made my head light, she made me twitch. The blood in my extremities seemed to run cool through my system. I entangled my fingers in and through her hair and pulled her down, deeply inserting myself past her tonsils and into her throat. She enjoyed it. I could feel her smiling lips. She began to rub my chest with passionate hot hands. I felt like a Man.

This type of treatment is only deserving of two types of guys. One of which I just identified myself as, a Man (that masculine force women love.) or that dude who pays for the act.

I got high off of the scenario, my nerves got sensitive. I released one hand and slid it down her back and unbuckled her bra in a one, two move like a pro. She sat up and took the bra off completely. I could see that it was her titties givin' the bra its shape, not the bra givin' the shape to her titties. They were a woman's pipe dream. I let go of her hair, it fell. I cupped her blessings as she devoured mines.

She had me open metaphorically. I guess I had her open too, at least one part of her. It wasn't long before I had another part of her open as well. The first body part I entered her with was my tongue. I told you she had me open. I was feelin' her in ways I can't feel myself. Call me a moderate narcissist. I went there and lapped her pussy up like a dog at a bowl of milk with a mouth full of peanut butter. At that point in time I wouldn't argue the possibility of being caught up in the moment. But as our relationship progressed, the congeniality of our souls implied that the intensity ran deeper.

She straddled me, I slid into her. She was wet, several temperatures past warm and ready. It was like capturin' the humidity of a hot day in Miami out of the atmosphere and containin' it in a small carnal canal. I melted. She dripped sweet honey. I thrust up into her. She hugged my head and smothered me with her soft, sweet, slippery, supple sacks. I held my breath and pumped her from the bottom. Her body responded with a tighter grip. Her hips began to grind and swivel on my dick. Her skin got more and more moist. I could feel sweat lubricatin' the friction between our skin.

My hands moved under her arms, up her back until I could grip her shoulders. As I pumped, I pulled her down onto me until I hit somethin' hidden on the back wall in her special place. She sprung up erect. I took a breath. Her cum smelled like somethin' I would want to butter a biscuit with. We heard a noise. She dug her head into the side of my neck and froze. Neither one of us moved an inch or made a sound. It was a guy walkin' through. Luckily, we were in the corner in the dark on a dark couch. Our skin color performed the characteristic of a chameleon, camouflagin' with the dark. When we were sure he was gone I rolled over and laid her on her back, never comin' out of the hive where my nectar was in surplus. I took her hands and stretched them high over her head, along the length of the couch as my dick stretched along the length of her pussy walls. I shot deep strokes with my body restin' fully on top of hers. She began to moan. I covered her lips with my mouth. The deeper I dug, the more pressure I had to put on her lips. The harder I hit it, the more she attempted to scream in ecstasy. The more she matched my rhythm, the more sweat developed. Her hands slipped out of mines. She pushed my lips off hers and said,

"I can feel the veins in your dick! I'm Cummin'!"

First it started in my legs then my butt cheeks got tight. My balls began tinglin'. She moaned into my ear. My skin raised and my eyesight left me briefly. Her legs wrapped around mines. We kept grindin'. You could hear the smackin' sound comin' from down below. My hands spread open wide like my fingers stopped gettin' along. I became incoherent to the point where I didn't give a fuck about nothin'. You could've gone in my pockets and took all my money right then. Her breathin' got erratic. Then Boom! She imploded. Boom! I exploded. The squishy, squishy mixture of our fluids kept me hard though I was done. Never in my life have I ever understood so clearly why so often so many people mistake good sex for love.

The next time I had an opportunity to witness her beauty was a rendezvous we had scheduled for 9 o'clock at Liemert Park. She joined me in the intimacy of the two-seater, European design that served as our transportation for the night. I told her she could leave her car for free at the meter until 7am because it was after hours. There would be no charge, so there was no need to even glance towards the ash tray. I call it the cash tray because cigarettes are unauthorized, blunt ashes go out the window. Only the remnants that fall from paper money are discarded into the tray. Coins (minus pennies) start with a "C" and they are the ash of spent bills, that's why I call it the cash tray. But to continue on with the story, me and her continued on to the Hacienda Hotel. It is a hotel accustomed to dealin' with new arrivals flyin' into LAX and requestin' to be shuttled to a place of close proximity as well as above par standards. For once I spent no time dazzlin' my prey with all the amenities the hotel had to offer. We went right to the room.

I did fail to mention that we made a stop by my boy's house (we call him Fingers, don't ask me why.) because he had six bottles of Moet champagne in his trunk, well actually my trunk because we had switched cars earlier in the day. I retrieved two of them. He had a hot girl with him that was involved in the music industry pretty heavy. Now that I think about it, he met her at my birthday party. She was a friend of a friend. He was my Roll Dawg, and as Roll Dawgs do, he followed me to the hotel with his soulmate for the night. Me and my lovely one still went right to our room. My homeboy got the suite next door and they were adjoined. Since that was the case and me being sociable amongst women and friends, I took her next door to socialize.

Unknown to the women, me and him were doin' what we do, havin' a beauty and brain contest between the women and a playa of the day contest for me and him. I won't say who won because we both probably think we did. Between the four of us we emptied the two bottles. Me and Fingers disintegrated a blunt of some sticky, icky light green. The whole time we lounged in his suite, I teased my lust, knowin' what guilty pleasure I could be indulgin' in instead. She caught me lookin' at her. The picture in her eyes told me somethin' that added up to a thousand words. In my words, it said we were on the same wavelength, her desires paralleled mines. She wanted to know what my sex was like on a big bed, on the floor and on the balcony in the moon light. Subconsciously, she wanted to have to go get her obviously, freshly done hair, done over again the next day. She was bubbly from the champagne, still she sat conservatively, not realizin', it's unrealistic to think that you can contain the eminence of natural sex appeal. Her inhibitions were losin' the battle against the 20% alcohol by volume. I kept teasin' my lust. Then she spoke in another language. She uncrossed her legs, then, re-crossed them the other way. It was body language. She excused herself and went to our room. She was sayin' that she didn't want to play my game with me, that games were for kids anyway and that she was ready to act like grown-ups. I stayed about ten more minutes and continued shootin' the shit about nothin' in particular. It played out fast.

I decided that it was time to go to my room and play with my toy. She was in the bathroom, the door was open, she was lotionin' up after a shower. I peeked in while she was bent over with her left foot on the edge of the tub, givin' attention to her left leg, below the knee. I snuck back over to the other side of the room when I heard her comin'. She stepped over the threshold with a burgundy silk robe, stickin' to her like new flesh. I traded rooms with her and took a shower. As the water rained down over my head, somethin' happened.

Either my mind was playin' tricks on me due to inebriation or I had a moment of clarity within my intoxication. I was transcended to the beginnin', showerin' under a waterfall. I felt the anticipation Adam felt preparin' for the second time he would have sex with Eve. When I exited the bathroom, she was layin' on her stomach, in the nude, on the bed with her feet in the air. She was readin' through summaries on the TV screen for Movies on Demand. Then she pushed a button on the remote and picked one, even though she knew we wouldn't see it. To my surprise, it was a movie called "Heat." my favorite movie.

How did she know?

Her body was a few shades lighter than her face. It was the color of unadulterated cocoa butter. I critiqued it. Incredible! Only thing I could think was that she must have done everythin' that God asked of her in a prior life and this time he rewarded her with one of the finest vehicles to get around in. She had mountains and bumps like a strip of motorcross raceway. I felt like she was my reward from the Game God for being a hell of a hustla in this life.

I had my artificials on, meanin', I had done two hundred pushups in the bathroom and my muscles were on temporary swole. I had stroked my little slugger a bit, so he was primed up and hangin' on swole too, but not erect. She had a lot to assess when her eyes landed on me. In addition to my heart throb masculinity, my skin told a story with tattoos.

It wasn't a quick story either, seein' that they covered my arms, chest, stomach, back and legs. We didn't talk about it but the story told her that I was entrenched in the Thug Life by way of being a Lost Angel. I could tell it enhanced her intrigue and raised questions as to who I was really, but there were no questions, only answers that night. All night she kept sayin' "Yes! Yes! Yes!"

I felt her skin and it was cool to the touch. It made me think about makin' her sweat. I started on my journey to conceive Cain and Abel. I rubbed her arm from the wrist up to her shoulder with a slow, slight touch. My palm slid across her skin like a silk sheet. I saw her hairs stand up on small mountains across the landscape of her flesh.

A couple more rubs made her skin respond, reciprocatin' heat. Her peach fuzz hairs laid back down. She turned her head to look up at me, smiled and rolled over on her back. Her left hand went up the back of my leg and she actually grabbed a handful of my butt and pulled towards her. I don't want to tell you that I felt violated because she's really pullin' my ass cheeks apart. I just fell into her to avoid further separation. I broke my fall with my elbow near her head. My lips landed right on hers. First they just sat there, fully on each other then hers began to suck slowly. Her tongue came sweepin' between, leavin' saliva in its wake. Now lubricated, she sucked my top lip into her mouth and played with it like a piece of gummy candy. I laid on top of her while she put both of my lips into her mouth. I tightened up the top one, she released it and got her fill off of the bottom one. Her body began to move beneath me. I matched her as if we were vertically positioned doing a sensual dance. She exhaled as I was inhalin'. Her breath went directly into my lungs. I got high off her poisonous vapors. Still I couldn't help but reminisce on the smell of her wet, waitin' and wantin' pussy, it smelled like somethin' that would draw ants, bees, bears and things like that. I don't think I would want to go campin' with her. She'd probably get eaten.

Tonight, I would do all the eatin'. I lifted off of her and went down low to re-fresh my memory of that comfortin' scent of her pussy. I put my nose into her hole and nodded my head yes extensively, as if I was in total agreement with what her pussy was whisperin' to me. She moaned when her nut cracked then she leaked into my mouth. The color reminded me of coconut juice. She tasted like it too. I love coconuts.

She told me to swing my body around onto her in a 69 position. As soon as my dick was within reach of her mouth, she gobbled it up, slobbered it up. She had one hand on my pubic hair area, pushin' my pelvis up. The other hand was on my butt, pullin' me back down into her mouth. She worked her way all the way back to my balls. She had my dick soooo wet. Then next thing I know she has my dick slidin' down the inside of her breast. She is actually holdin' her titties up with her biceps and her forearms are around my waist. Her hands palmed my ass once again. I jumped and caught goose bumps at what she did next. She gripped my ass and bathed my asshole with her tongue, chills raced from my feet to my head instantly. She almost made me moan like a girl. I felt sweat break out on the top of my head. She continued lappin' up my backside.

She was goin' bad. I didn't know how to think. My first thought was, Bitch, you better not tell nobody!

I imagined a person walkin' down the street on a scorchin' hot day with an ice cream cone meltin' down his arm. Her tongue put in more work than that. I couldn't take it no more, not because it didn't feel good enough or felt too good but because my manhood was tellin' me, "Man up and take control of the situation!" Once my manhood said that, I immediately changed positions. First I had to pop my butt cheeks out of her grasp though. I turned around and redeemed myself by climbin' onto her head and stuffin' her mouth full of dick. I went so deep she gagged.

Yeah, how you like that? Swallow this dick!

I put my feet flat on the bed and teabagged her, (squattin' like a sumo wrestler, lowerin' my balls down into her mouth.) Being gentle with my nuts is important. In my opinion, she imported them into her portal precisely. Squattin' is not one of my favorite exercises and I began to feel like I was workin' out so I came down on my knees and propped her head up with two pillows. The next thing she knew I was fuckin' her mouth like a Jack Rabbit. That created a lot of spit. She took it like a soldier but yet maintained her soft feminine essence. That had me so hard I was afraid I would get stretch marks on my dick.

I slowed my pace and watched it go in and out. Sometimes it would come out a lil dryer and sometimes it would come out completely laced with her saliva. I kept strokin' her while holdin' her head.

45

Slower, I slowed my groove. I went slow but deep. So deep, it was the deepest to the second power because I went as deep as she had room for, the deepest anyone has ever ventured.

"Uh oh!" She gagged!

"I'm sorry. You okay?"

"Damn Boy, whut you tryna do, make me swallow it?

"I'm sorry."

"That's enough of that, you gonna mess around and kill me. Just put it in my pussy."

Now she was speakin' my language. I'd rather marinate in some hot pussy than get head any day. But I had to see if she would go into slut mode for me and it seemed like we were off to a good start.

I climbed down her physique and buried my head into her buoyant breast. I had maneuvered down into the perfect spot. My face rolled in her soft pillow-like breast. The endorphins in my brain swam free like angels, enhanced by the hot moist sensation her soakin' wet pussy gave to the tip of my dickhead. Suddenly I slammed it in, she tried to jerk up off of me but I had her shoulders anchored down with my hands. She received her punishment without protest. Her beautiful facial features were balled up to a point where she wasn't beautiful anymore. I banged her incessantly, tears rolled out of the corners of her eyes. She dug her nails into my back while screamin' through clenched teeth that she was cummin'.

"I'm cummin' hard Baby! Damn, I'm cummin' so hard! Oooooooooh! Oh my God! Daaaamnnn! Oooooooooh."

I did a lot of things to her that night and you would've thought that all night, I was askin' her questions because all night, she kept yellin', "Yes!"

Sharply at 11am we got the check out time, phone call. We showered off each other's DNA and left. We didn't even stop to eat. She needed to get out of public. She was lookin' too recently well fucked. When we got to her car, the parkin' enforcer had left a ticket. I glanced at the cash tray. I asked her how much it was and handed her two twenty dollar bills. That one was on me.

Within a few weeks of being at her parent's house, she moved into a townhouse on the outskirts of L.A. The buildin' had two pools and two Jacuzzis that closed at ten o'clock. And if you know me you'd know I like to play in that water, from jet skis at the lake to the rubber duckie in the bathtub. I often retired in the confines of her buildin' by 9pm.

I'd swim ten laps in the pool then relieve myself of the stresses of the world in the spa, until the chubby white lady with the title of manager made her rounds. She never told me that I had to get out. It was her Kool Aid smile that told me that she liked chocolate that always signaled me that it was time to go in.

The aura of the apartment was always serene. Candles were her thing. She didn't like to listen to gangster rap or hip hop but she did love the thug in me. She often relaxed on the couch with the door open to enjoy the midnight air. Neo-Soul music filled the air like background music as she would have a glass or two of The Club Long Island Iced Tea. She didn't have a house phone and anytime her Nextel two-way would chirp it would be one of two of her girlfriends. It would take much less than a lucky guess at this point for you to figure out where and with who was high on my list of places to be and people to be with.

Time keeps on tickin'. Six months seemed to go by in two. One evenin' I attended a social gatherin' at her parent's house and met her sister whose body was stacked thick and rich like Miss Butterworth. She commanded my attention and caused my imagination to go on some vivid (what if?) escapades. She was with her fiance', a brother who had his stuff together, financially in the legal world. But all I could see was a victim, who if circumstances were different would have my hands in his, quite literally. So temptation for both parties of the couple existed but was easily suppressed as well because on this givin' Sunday I was satisfied in both areas.

I felt a genuine acceptance from her parents. They were down to earth and to me were a vision of me and her, a glimpse into the future. A couple that had made it out of the game, moved out of the hood, got the real house and had a relationship that was on one thousand. And that's on a scale from one to ten. I saw me headed in that direction. Who I would end up doin' it with was in the air, but the way things were goin', she easily fit in the wifey position of my aspiration. She fit so comfortably on my arm that I didn't mind takin' sand to the beach. (A violation of the rules for the novice players and a tactic for the more experienced playa while they throw back French Connections all night.) Cause invariably the club is full of fine women who want what your date has, you. I took her and her buddies to a few industry parties and introduced them to some heavy weights with un-depletable bank accounts. Like Gary Payton, Lil Jon and Michael Clark Duncan. That brother didn't look nearly as big as he did on Green Mile, when he played John Coffee, Coffee like the drink.

While he was on his best behavior, showing his teeth and doing what all egotistical male celebs do when in the presence of three attractive women, I sized 'im up.

I thought I could take 'im as long as I didn't let 'im dopefiend me in the back of the head like he did dude on "Player's Club".

The night was good as usual. Whenever the girls strangely but conveniently had to use the restroom all at the same time I made additions into my phonebook. It's in the blood. I'll bet you mustaches that... huh... yeah mustaches. If you lose I get to shave yours off.

I bet you mustaches that my forefathers had multiple women. I know my father did because I have two other siblings the same age as me. My father has a brother and a sister the same age. And just to be of absolute clarity there are no twins among the aforementioned. Plus it's my civic duty to combat the ratio injustice of 10 to 1 women to men. So you can understand the disparity in equality when I spend so much time with my still new pussy after workin' on it and playin' in it for halfway down the calendar.

We spent many weekends in hotels. Sometimes it would be like, "Listen, I'm in Dallas or Atlanta. There's a ticket for you at the airport, fly out here I'ma shake my homies and lock up with you in a suite." Other times it would be her job sendin' her as a Rep. to attend conventions. Her position allowed her all expense paid trips with which she would cater to me lavishly. All I needed to do was get there. One time I'll never forget, she was stayin' at the Marriot close by in Anaheim. The valet opened my truck door and I grabbed a few hangers with plastic draped over a few outfits fresh from Men's Land except for the pit stop to be pressed at the cleaners. Then my Louis Vuitton carryin' case equipped with the Prada cologne, lotion and deodorant. Toothbrush, toothpaste, hair pomade and brush to make sure my waves faded smooth as a calm tide in the midnight hour at Santa Monica Beach. As the concierge took my belongings and a twenty dollar tip to carry them to my... her... I mean, the company's room, he told me that she was in the restaurant at the bar waitin' for me.

She sat on a bar stool with her legs crossed at the ankles sippin' on what was no doubt a Long Island Iced Tea. I slid my hand around her neck up the back of her head through her silky hair and pressed her lips to mines and threw my tongue down her throat. I savored the taste of her sweetness mixed with the Long Island. Just as I was taking a seat next to her, the bartender sat on the counter a quarter glass of Hennessey VSOP in a brandy snifter diagonally on top of a full glass of hot water then he did the same with a quarter glass of Grand Marnier. She looked at me with an expression that said, "if you're going to do it, do it fa' real." That's the good thing about being in a nice place with experienced people. I learned that warm liquor was smoother in two ways. One was that it went down your throat smoother and two that it acclimated to your body temperature easier for a smoother reaction to the liquor. I am now officially a half ass French Connection connoisseur.

We went to the room with a buzz in full swing. I took a shower to wash the day off of me. I dabbed myself with cologne in a few choice spots, like my chest and ears to subtly stimulate her other senses, like smell while I primarily stimulated her sensation of touch. 260 pushups later I pimp walked out the bathroom wearin' only Sean John boxer briefs and a wife beater. Her Colgate commercial audition smile turned into "What the fuck is that?!!!"

Hold up, them ain't the right lines.

She was comin' closer focusin' in on my neck.

"A hickey Punk?!"

Oh shit! I completely forgot about that. The day before, one of my miscellaneous females had went old school on me and tagged me with a passion mark. She told me to leave the room. I was straight up wrong, so I left.

Bad luck and misfortune. Ohh man, the ramifications of not havin' your shit tight. Good luck I was only an hour away from L.A. in Anaheim. Fortunately, I had a girlfriend in Buena Park the next city over and fifteen minutes away. I called her from her driveway. She told me to come inside. I told her to come outside. I was still deliberatin' on my next move and didn't want to commit myself by crossin' the threshold of her lair. She got into the truck and held my hand and talked to me. I listened to me reprimand myself for being so game goofy. I consulted my status symbol/bitch eye catcher that had a secondary function of a time piece. Forty minutes had passed since I left the hotel. She put her hand on her favorite part of me. She could tell somethin' troubled me and offered to make it all better. I kissed her and told her I had to go.

I left and called the hotel and was transferred to the room. She was still cryin'. She made me promise to be more considerate and asked if I wanted to come back. She had me open plus I pride myself on my high percentage of things going accordin' to plan, and I had planned on being in Anaheim for the weekend.

Over the course of our physically and mentally stimulatin' past timin', we also had a few insignificant clashes. I had come to find out that she was very opinionated and head strong. Not that I think that's a bad thing because it takes a strong man to keep a strong woman in her place. It's just that sometimes in the contentious atmosphere it would seem to me to be an intellectual superiority and power struggle. I could always recognize when the debate wasn't about the insignificant topic. Then I would either trump the situation or cause a stand off by pullin' my who's feelin' who or who has who open more than who, card. I did that in different ways but most effectively. I would put several miles between us.

On more than one occasion we went for a few weeks before we would succumb to the compellin' force to rendezvous to fill her void and my need to fit in. But it wasn't just physical. We were compatible in a lot of areas, maybe alike in too many. A month long hiatus ended on the night of the Chuck Liddel vs Rashad Evans fight. I was on the block instructin' a 14yr old hustler who was on the straight and narrow, at least so far at this point in his life, on how to properly care for the leather interior of my Towncar.

I was also watchin' my homies get their $200 jeans dirty, while bettin' a thousand dollars that a certain number will land on the dice in a possibility of three combinations, against the possibilty of the number seven landin' in a combination of three ways, when she called me to inquire what the bizness was.

Said she was at Magic Johnson's Fridays with one of her homegirls and a female business associate from the company's division in Texas. I told her my intentions were to hit The House Of Blues on Sunset to watch the fight when I was free from my current situation. I didn't tell her that it was mostly the bubonic chronic that had me in a stupor for the last thirty minutes, knowin' the fight had already started. She asked me to come to her while she checked with the girls about movin' the party to Hollywood. One of my boys who was more interested in kickin' it with some women than the chance of subsidizin' his out a town hustle with everyone else's out a town hustle money rollin' dice, went with me.

There ain't nothin' like goin' to see a fine female in a new car with heated seats and a pocket full of money, high on some potent dozha to make you feel like breakin' the law was worth every risk. I called to tell her that I was in the parkin' lot while I was temporarily mesmerized by the fat behind on a white girl as she approached two black girls. One of the black girls had a cell phone to her ear. She was sayin', "I'm in the parkin' lot too."

My mind clicked back to face recognition mode. My brain was registerin' slow but I told you I was high.

She saw the car and came to me. Two of 'em got in with us while the phenomenal associate got into a Jeep and pulled up behind us. I turned the music up loud to the lyrics of J-Hova cause I was feelin' like the man upstairs my damn self right then. I weaved in and out of traffic up La Cienega Blvd. effortlessly. We made a right on Sunset. The House Of Blues was packed, the valet was full. But I learned a long time ago there is always room for one more for a fifty dollar handshake, in this case I made two handshakes. Then they taxed me at the door fifty dollars a head, you do the math, a bunch of fives, it's easy plus two cars in valet $350 to watch a fight that had to be damn near over and watchin' it on TV at that.

I don't give away money to look big, I give it away to live good. Livin' good would be the possibility of a me'nage a' trois. But my chick is the jealous type, so that ain't goin' down regardless if I slipped her two ecstasy pills. We went to the bar, she pulled out her corporate credit card and ordered two bottles of Dom P. She told the bartender to have a waitress find us a table upstairs where the big screens were. She told me that she was expected by the company to finance a wonderful experience over the week for her visitin' associate.

A thought came to mind. It was that she should've pulled out the card roughly ten minutes prior. She said she couldn't explain payin' $250 to get into The House of Blues without someone performin' live on stage. She had a point. The associate lookin' like an older version of Stevie from The Parkers, came up and told her to go to the Ladies room with her. But she was seriously close to me. She even put her hand on my chest to brace herself when someone squeezed through the crowd. My girl looked at me, I looked at Stevie, My girl looked at Stevie, Stevie looked nonchalant. They went to the restroom.

We were seated at a booth where we could see the rest of Chuck Liddel gettin' knocked out like he owed dude some money. I saw some playas I knew rockin' their ball caps to the side and drinkin' French Connections. They acknowledged that I was encased by three women with my boy on the end whisperin' raw and uncut game into her homegirl's ear. As luck would have it my girl and the white girl were sittin' on either side of me. Since the white girl was talkative and the only other person she knew prior to this evenin' was sittin' on the other side of me, I got a lot of "inadvertant" physical attention, from the feet touchin', the knees bumpin', elbows, everythin'. It didn't go unnoticed but I was innocent and ready to plead not guilty. When the fight was over, half the club emptied out. We drank two more bottles of DP and played around on the dance floor to jams like Cutie Pie and More Bounce.

After about an hour of that, we were ready to go. While me and my girl stood at the bar pickin' up her credit card she reminded me that her love was all mines and that she wanted some identical reciprocation. She repeated herself but with different words then it dawned on me that she was giving me an ultimatum. That was the first time that I thought that she was really all I needed to be happy. I had missed her the last 33 days, 12 and a half hours. I contemplated it while I took my boy home. The girls went back to Fridays to pick up her coupe. I met her at her house.

Passion is undeniably the most valuable intangible tangible a human being can experience.

I touched her with the sensitivity that you possess when you emotionally receive someone into your heart. I psychologically accepted that I had played the hand that all playas prayed to play, the hand that allowed you to put your player's card up.

I kissed and licked her from the top of her head to the bottom of her personality. The music played in the background, the soundtrack to our personal movie. Ha! Two main characters with no speakin' roles. I didn't need R Kelly to tell me it wasn't nothin' wrong with a lil bump n' grind. Our clothes were scattered across the livin' room. The floor was in disarray like a teenager's bedroom. We took it from the couch to the bed to the floor and back to the couch to the floor (I would say kitchen counter, dinner table and patio but that's not what really happened) and back to the bed. The last orgasm expended the last of the energy we had. We were maxed out like a stolen credit card.

I don't know what time it was, my watch was on the floor in the livin' room somewhere. The CD changer was still playin' songs at random. Heather Headly was on and yeah, I felt like a pleasure releaser, a make her believer, a bad times undoer and a joy bringer. For the umpteenth time I thought there was no place I'd rather be and no one I'd rather be there with. I had taken my sedative and had administered her a generous dosage. We were out for the count of ten and beyond. What happened next had me and still has me fucked up.

It was maybe 3 o'clock in the mornin'. We were both startled by someone bangin' on the door and yellin' her name. He was obviously irritated, maybe because we were so far out of it that we didn't hear his first attempt.

"Akira! Akira!"

I looked at her like, "Who tha fuck is that yellin' your name and why aren't you answerin'."

I stated exactly what I was thinkin'. She laid there quiet. I imagine she was blinkin' her eyes like "I dream of Jeannie" tryin' to make him disappear or maybe she was tryin' to make me disappear. I'm a bit disoriented but I doubt I'm dreamin'. Then there was silence outside for a few minutes. There was silence from her. Everythin' was quiet except in my mind.

The bangin' and yellin' started up again. In hindsight I guess he went to the underground parkin' to see if her car was there. This time she got up and went out of the room. I got up too. I was wearin' my birthday suit. She came back tyin' up her robe and handed me my boxers. By now I could hear that he was fuckin' with the window. It's a scary situation because I'm vulnerable and this dude is determined.

She said somethin' to him like, "Why are you messing with my window?"

Now I'm fartin' because she said it at a volume that made it evident there was no partition between them impedin' her voice.

Then she said, "I have company."

Oh shit! There was a loud noise. The blinds sounded like they came off of their hinges. I knew he was inside and I knew where he was headed.

MY GUN IS IN THE FUCKIN' CAR!!!!!

I pushed the bedroom door closed to just a crack and scanned the room for a weapon, anythin', I was desperate. I assessed everythin' in the room in a second or two. A clothes hanger on the floor, I almost picked it up. A cardboard box full of clothes, the comforter on the bed, a wicker chair, a 17 inch television on top of a small table. I damn near went for the TV. I'm sure he always dreamed of havin' his face on TV but it was across the room and right then I was in the best spot possible, positioned behind the door.

The last object I saw was the best. On the floor, two feet away was an iron.

Oh yeah she did always iron in the bedroom. It's always in here somewhere.

I grabbed it. It fit in my hand like a $5,000 stack of $100 bills. All this happened in less than three seconds. My brain was workin' overtime in problem solvin' mode and had commanded that plenty adrenaline be pumped into my system.

He came burstin' into the room.

Booom!!!

Even though the iron wasn't plugged up I tried to straighten out his mind through his forehead.

Bam!!!

Good thing it was him and not her who came through the door first.

I hit him with the edge of the iron and opened up his face, then I bashed him again with the influence of the chemical runnin' through my veins. The iron shattered into a thousand pieces. He dropped and I was on top of him. I grabbed him how the wrestlers do when gettin' ready to power drive their opponent. But I had no intention of that. I was just holdin' him down workin' off of instinct. I took a quick assessment. This dude was every bit of 6'3" 240 lbs. Big feet, fully dressed. But he was dazed. I had momentary control. I had to maintain it. Remainin' how we were positioned until he regained some type of composure was not an option.

I tried to get up. He grabbed me by the boxers. I know he felt like one of Tyson's opponents in his prime after they hit the canvas from one of two of those blows that earned him the name Iron Mike. I tried to get up two more times, two more times he didn't let me. His blood was streamin' out and makin' things real messy real fast.

In another try I pushed him down and jerked away from him at the same time. I ran to the dishwasher and grabbed two knives. In my opinion one was too small but I had a big one too that held his big ass at bay. He picked up her cell phone and barked into it.

"Ay Cuzz come back! It was a nigga in the house! Cuzz come now!"

He didn't approach me, he was helpless. I was confused.

Who the fuck is this fool? How far away is his homies?

Who is this bitch really?

I'm standin' in the livin' room with two knives in my hand and nothin' but boxers on my ass. I shook the spot like a earthquake, ran outside and around a few corners of the maze of the complex to hide from dude's homies. It was just me. I didn't know him or her. It took me about thirty seconds to realize that what I was doin' wasn't goin' to work. It was too late at night and I was too far away from home. An hour away in my situation was like being on the moon. All my clothes and car keys were inside. I walked back inside luckily the door was still open. My attitude was up high along with my blades.

"I ain't no bitch ass nigga! Let's get that straight, even though I just ran up outta here like a bitch. You run up on me I'ma make steak and rib tips out yo big ass!"

My chest is exposed so he can plainly see that I was branded with the tales of the street.

He asked me, "Where you from?"

I told him, "Don't ask me no questions! Ask yo bitch where she been!"

I picked up and threw on my clothes piece by piece while I kept one eye on him. He asked me how long I been fuckin' her. That was one question that told me that he thought her love and legs belonged to him, just like I did. I told him he really didn't want to know but my mind was on somethin' else and racin'. His boys are on their way and most logically the police because the buildin' was predominately white.

I'm spazzin' inside my head because I can't find my keys and I've already looked in the same place two or three times. He asked me if she told me about him. I don't know if he was tryin' to satisfy his ego or if he was tryin' to determine who was more at fault, her for infidelity or me for manipulatin' a woman who told me she had a man. By this time she had called his name and I recognized it from her "liberal" expressions of being open about the past and experiences with her former boyfriends.

"Yeah but she said she left yo broke ass and the tired relationship before I met her." I said sarcastically.

That boiled his blood. He ran to the sink to get himself a knife. But as usual everythin' was in the dishwasher. It was obvious he hadn't spent much time there. But it was also obvious he was touched by her betrayal. He slapped her again for the fourth or fifth time. I wasn't countin'. She accepted them like she knew she was wrong. She deserved much more. I had to come dangerously close to him. (dangerous for him if he flinched) to get my bracelet and Sidekick

LX phone off of the kitchen counter. When I started back to continue my search for my keys I saw them peekin' out from under the couch. I smiled. I'm outta here. He was asking her somethin' about how she could do him like that, I didn't mean to interrupt, well, okay I really did.

I said, "Oh yeah, she sucks good dick and you might wanna be gentle til her asshole heals up."

He shrieked, "Ahhh! You bitch ass nigga!" and grabbed a chair from the dinette set and chunked it at me. It slammed into the door on my way out. His phone was on the window ledge outside. I took it. I sprinted down the stairs and to my car like a cat in the night. I pushed the keyless entry button from about fifty feet and saw the headlights blink and interior lights come on. I could hear sirens in the air. Thank God the security gate opened automatically from the inside. I pulled out and made a right turn on the main street. Once I got about two hundred yards up I saw one, two... three, four police cars turn off the main street ahead and come my way. I looked in the rearview and saw about three cars worth of strobe lights behind me. The four cars ahead of me zoomed past me. The cars behind me turned into the buildin'. There were about fifteen seconds too late to determine if the unsuspicious Executive edition Lincoln Towncar was leavin' the scene or merely passin' through.

The next day I scrolled through the A's in his phone to call her and tell her that I had his phone and that I left my other phone there but I couldn't find her name. I dialed her number and pushed send. Her number was already programmed under the name Wifey.

LOVE IS A DISEASE
I'M
KEEPIN' IT PLAYA

Then I decide to find some freak nasty writers from around the country. I was in Atlanta so I started there. I held a contest amongst the underground writers of Atlanta. The experience was crazy. I met all types. What I liked most were the dirty minded women that were more than willin' to open up to me, if you know what I mean. Well shit, this is an erotica book so I can talk to you. It's just between me and you right? Aight, there was this one chick, well she was more like a bitch, a nasty bitch, a fine ass intellectual nasty ass bitch. She showed up to my room with a notebook. I was at a hotel in downtown Atlanta, the Marriot Marquis, damn near top floor. The shit cost me a grip. I still haven't paid my credit card bill for that. But anyway, she comes in with this trench coat on and this attitude like she knows she's about to get the spot in the book. She starts readin' this story where she starts off gettin' fucked upside down in the ass. My dick got hard immediately. I tried to contain myself, then the story got more and more erotic and as the story got more erotic she came out of her coat and you know she had on her birthday suit underneath right? Then there's this scene in her story where she gets out of the shower and walks over to her man who's sittin' on the bed. Okay, I'm sittin' on the bed. And she's walkin' over to me as she's readin'. My little G.I. Joe is a fully trained Iraqi soldier right about now and he's aimin' his rocket launcher right at her. At some point, I wasn't hearin' the story anymore. She climbed on top of me and we got it goin' at full speed for about two hours.

After we fell out flat on the bed exhausted and sweaty, she continued to read her story. The story got scary on me. It took a wild turn for the worst. Suddddenly, the girl in the story started cuttin' the man up with a razor she had in her mouth. She sliced his dick off and this girl had devilish grin on her face while she was readin' the stuff. I got scared! I had to think of somethin' fast, so I called room service. I wanted somebody to come to the room. I didn't wanna order food because it would take too long and this bitch was gettin' more and more excited. At first she was layin' on her side readin'. Now she was sittin' up and looked like she was about to get up on her feet. I asked room service for some towels. I told 'em that the bath tub had overflowed and that I needed the towels fast. The deranged freak didn't understand why I was lyin'.

When I hung up the phone I told her that we had to get dressed before room service got to the room. She didn't understand what was goin' on but she got dressed and so did I. When the lil Mexican lady came in with the towels I told her to come in. Then I acted like I liked the story so much that I wanted everybody to hear it. I told the girl to read it for the maid.

She said, "She don't even understand English."

I said, "Read it to her anyway!"

She got an attitude. I got an attitude too. I told her I had somewhere I had to go. I walked her to her car. Damn! I was happy to get rid of her.

I interviewed some more authors at different places at different times and Blackman was the best, hands down with 10 page sex scenes. His story is named Yum Yum.

The Adventures of

Yum Yum

by

Brock D. Blackman

© 2017

<u>Getting Schooled</u>

I heard a horn blow from the other side of the street as a car pulled up. It was Val in my mother's car. She rolled down the window.

"Lawrence, you need a ride home baby?" she asked, emphasizing "ride."

Alex was on me when he saw her.

"Yo L. Who's ma?"

"My mom's friend." I told him. I turned to her and said, "Yeah Val."

"What's up with her?" he asked me.

"Nothing." I told him.

I asked her if we could give him a ride home. She didn't mind. We jumped in and she sped off. When we pulled up to Alex's house,

Marisol came out trying to see who was in their drive way. She probably thought it was one of her men. Dang, that woman was fine. Alex jumped out giving me a pound and said, "Tomorrow, aight?"

"No question." I murmured staring past him at Marisol. She was grinning madly now that she saw that it was her victim. She waved. I waved back. Alex looked at me.

"You know my sister?"

"Not really. I met her when I came over that time to tell you about the party."

"The party?" he eyed me suspiciously.

"The party I couldn't warn you about because you wasn't home."

"Oh." he relaxed. "Well stay away from her. She ain't no good."

He bounced into his crib. Val pulled out. She questioned me as she drove. "You like her?"

I didn't know what to say.

"It's okay. I'm not jealous but I can see it in your eyes. You and her go through something?"

"Almost." I muttered.

"Oh," she laughed. "she's the one."

"Yeah, she's the one."

"Well, what happened?"

"You don't want to know."

"Sure I do. I wouldn't have asked if I didn't want to know."

"She ah... She ah, she beat me for my head." I told her.

"Huh?" she asked, not clear of my meaning.

I explained how Marisol had taken advantage of my inexperience and had me lick her low while I got nothing in return, but a craving to do it again.

Val laughed. "Now I'm jealous."

"For what? You're the one who took my virginity."

She pouted, looking hurt. "Why didn't you lick me low?"

"You didn't let me."

"Shit, you didn't try. You can eat this pussy anytime."

"Is that so?" I said looking at her.

"Any time you want to suck this thang, you can." she sassed as we pulled up to the house.

"You ready now?" I pressed her.

"Boy, don't play with me."

"Girl, ain't nobody playing with you. What? You scared?" I taunted.

"Scared? That reverse psychology shit don't work on me. If I wanted your head, I'd do like Marisol and take it." she told me as she got out the car.

I got out and followed her into the house.

"You ain't got to take it. I'm offering it to you." I grabbed her hand and turned her around. I looked down at her. "What's up?"

"Boy, you're going to get yourself into something you can't handle."

"Seems like I handled it fine Saturday."

"Saturday shouldn't have happened."

"But it did. What's up?" I said again putting my arms around her, cupping her butt with my hands.

"Alright now. Don't be starting nothing you can't finish."

"If I start it, I'll finish it." I shot back at her.

Using her soft curves as handles to pull her to me I leaned down to kiss her. I rubbed the supple flesh up and down and around, squeezing the Charmin. Our lips met and I knew from the charge that she was as eager as I was. I pushed her against the wall. She slipped out of my arms breaking our kiss.

"Alright now." She said grabbing my wrist. "You done started it. Now you're going to finish it."

She led me to my room. I followed watching her butt swish side-to-side calling to me. "Kiss me, lick me, frisk me."

Inside I locked the door and hurriedly stripped. She stood watching me undress. I finally pulled off my boxers, my Johnson was alert and standing firm. It wavered from side to side as if searching for she whom had aroused him from his slumber.

"Damn!" she said eyeing me. "I thought you wanted to eat this pussy, not beat this pussy."

"Eat it. Beat it. It don't matter."

"Yes it does." she informed me, beginning to unbutton her blouse.

She stripped down to the skin she was born in. Her body was well toned and soft in all the right places. I'd been too caught up the first time to fully admire and appreciate her.

"Damn, you're beautiful." I let her know.

I went to her. She welcomed me with a kiss.

Together we sank to my bed, Val guiding me with her lips. I planted my hot brand on her neck down to her throat. She fingered and traced the contours of my arms and back, feeling my structure and build. I kissed and licked her highs, loving her lows, and back to her peaks. I sucked each into my mouth so I could flick them with my tongue. She encouraged me by rubbing and testing my back for strength to support what was to come. I lowered my affections to pave a way to her navel and below. Then further south, her legs yawning wide to give me unrestricted access. That funky stuff punched me in the nose, with one aromatic whiff, challenging me to a duel. I accepted and licked my lips in preparation for my attack. I advanced. Her hands held the sides of my head guiding me to where I should be. My hands came to my assistance, clumsily parting her and going straight for the money. I lapped at her like a pup at its water bowl.

After a few moments she pulled my head up. I thought I was doing something. Her expression told me otherwise.

"Baby, let me show you how to do this."

She moved under me telling me to roll over on my back. She put a pillow under my head and told me to watch her carefully. She went down, crouched over me, and eyed my staff, which was eyeing her. She closed a hand around me.

"Watch how tender and attentive I am."

I watched. Her pouting cherry lips kissed my tip. She did it so softly it was like a ghost brushed me. It sent tendrils of thrill down to my toes. Like it was a Tootsie Pop, she put her lips around my pumped up head, twirling her tongue around the portion in her mouth. The tingle was killing me. Then it got better. She slowly inhaled him, showering him with her mouth. Up she came, sucking the excess off. Moving him to the side slightly, she licked its length from the top to the base, sucking one of my nuts in her mouth and pulling away until it popped from her lips. She sucked me in her mouth humming like it was magically delicious, but she had the lucky charm. She bobbed all the way up and down twice, then slower again. She was killing me. She pulled it out.

"You like that baby?"

"Yeah that's all good." I panted.

She went back at it, licking my length again, now around the base and all of a sudden, around my ass. My cheeks clenched as I sensed. She laughed.

"You see how I don't miss anything and try everything?"

I nodded wishing she wouldn't stop to talk.

"That's how you have to be with a woman, soft with pressure, attentive and exploring. You have to use your fingers more though. You have to love a woman's whole body, not just what's between her legs. Kiss and suck it. Lick and stick it. Caress every part of her your hands can touch. But most of all, you have to love her and love it while you're doing it. Feel her responses and ride her waves. Her body will tell you what she needs. You just have to listen, okay?"

"Alright." I panted almost breathlessly.

"You ready?"

"You ain't gonna finish?" I asked, wanting my nut.

"I thought you were going to finish what you started?"

"You finish what you started." I told her. "I was almost about to nut."

"Lesson Two. It's always ladies first, remember that boy!" she said putting me in my place.

We switched places. Once again between her twin welcoming committees, I kissed her columns. One at a time I admired and loved the contrasting supple softness and firmness of her legs. I lovingly made love to her legs one at a time, from the base down to the ankles. I held them high, kissing behind her knees, her hamstrings, on down to her butt. I kneaded them like dough with my fingers, tasting every inch of them. Between my journey from one leg to the other, I'd tease her by licking around her mound on each side, lightly kissing the top through her hair, and then I'd move on. I could feel her winding up as her body moved with my affections, squirming under my touch. I could feel her anxiousness building. Her cat was calling me as if it had fingers hooked in my nose pulling me. I came to its call. Using my fingers I massaged the sides of her mound where they met her legs.

Her lips moved the sides of her mound where they met her legs. Her lips moved with my fingers as if they were trying to smile and frown at the same time. I kissed her sideways smile and licked one mighty slash between her lips. Her hips rose as I licked her split from bottom to top. Ummm, she tasted good. I retreated a bit to catch my breath. She grabbed my ears, raising her hips to meet my lips. I kissed and sucked as she wound her hips into my mouth. By her soft moans I could tell she was enjoying her toy. I enjoyed being her boy.

When she settled down I used my tongue to lift and suck a lip into my mouth. I licked the inside of her fold and gave it the love and attention the last labia majora on earth deserved. I parted her sea of love to lick the inside of the other. I could almost see her moisten even more under my touch. I could definitely feel and taste the difference. Stiffening my tongue, I searched for her tunnel. Finding it I entered, keeping my tongue firm, drawing it out I licked upward, basting her entire core lightly with my probe. As I lashed it around, I hit a swollen lump. Her back arched.

"Aw, damn Baby. You got it. You got it baby." she whispered. "That's the clit. Get it Baby."

I licked it again, invoking the same response from her body. Supporting myself on my left elbow, I put my right arm around her left leg so my fingers would rest on top of her patch. I spread her lips with my thumb and pointer. Sucking two fingers on my left hand, I eased them into her. Pressing up into her I moved them in and out slowly and put my mouth over her clit and sucked gently on it. I moved my fingers in and out of her, rotating them and pressing them against her walls, constantly licking and sucking her sex. She bucked her body and her thighs clasped around my head with light pressure. Her hands palmed the back of my head, mashing me into her winding hips.

"Sssss. Ummm. That's it Baby." she moaned a whisper as I moved my fingers in her. "Up just a little more. Now over a little. Right there." she instructed me. "Now curl your fingers a little and stroke right there."

My curling fingers hit a spot with a slightly different texture to it. Her back arched almost lifting her body off the bed.

"Mmmm, ungh." she murmured.

I did it again. Her hands left my head to grab handfuls of sheets. I rubbed it again and again flattening my tongue on her clit, wiggling it with a steady pressure. She put her hands back on my head, mashing my face into her box like she was trying to smother me with her love. Her moans turned to inhaled hisses as I sucked her clit and rubbed her inner walls, now licking all over her wetness, savoring her taste. She began to shake and quiver. Her feet planted themselves and she laughed her hips at me. My lips clamped on her clit sucking strongly. My fingers triggered her spot as she came, spewing forth a musky fluid around my fingers and mouth. I lapped it up as it came, until she fell back exhausted. Her taste was the sweetest thing in the world! I tried to keep up my affections, but she pushed me from between her legs, closing them and moving them back and forth against each other like she had to pee and was holding it in.

Noooo! Not another Marisol, I thought. She must have read the expression on my face as I looked at her on the brink of panic.

"Give me a minute." she said breathlessly.

"Alright." I waited not knowing what else to do besides wonder if I'd gotten beaten for my head again.

She rolled onto her stomach as she regained her energy. Her legs opened slightly, her thighs flattened, and that ass bubbled up, looking plump and pretty. Maneuvering between her legs with my Johnson hard and aching for release, I began to kiss the back of her legs. I put a hand on each of her cheeks and massaged them; acting like it was dough in my hands. I kissed them to the crease, up and into their part. I spread them and her sex seemed to jump out at me, her lips puffy and standing out, glistening in her dark patch. There was a puddle of wetness under her from where she'd leaked her juices down to the sheets. I kissed her butt over and over tasting her hot cold sweat. She spread her legs to allow me easier access. I opened her halves and licked her from bottom to top and back to rim her. Her cheeks clenched and she jerked. I could tell she liked my tongue lashing. She rose a little on her knees. I went down and licked her lips. She wasn't so sensitive now, because she didn't move away. I slid a finger down between her lips, then another to spread her so

I could ease up into position. Using my fingers as a guide I mounted her, first rubbing my head around her to lubricate myself with her wetness. I slid into her feeling like I'd just glided into a pool of lava. If I was really chocolate I'd have surely melted inside her. Easing down until my pelvis met her butt, I pushed her to the bed flattening her butt I pressed myself fully into her. So excited and anxious was I that, after a few forays into her depths, I felt myself building up to my climax. Damn! I hit it a few more times and pulled out about to explode. My cum shot across the room like a projectile from a cannon as my member jerked and pulsed. I drained it and picked up where I'd left off; riding that ass. I mashed it up and down as I bounced on it. That pussy was so good it kept me hard. I pulled out just enough for me to rise over her legs as I closed them to straddle her, commencing my slow drive into her.

"Hold on a minute Baby." she told me.

I paused as she slid a pillow under her to raise her hips so I'd have better access to her. And did I! I stroked long, deep, and slow. Then three fast short strokes, now five or six long slow deep ones. Now fast. Then slow. She thrust back on me moaning her satisfaction. Our bodies met with a rhythmic Smack! Smack! as I timed myself to her thrusts. I locked my arms at the elbows and braced my body stiff so I could look down at me enter her sucking wetness. I was wet with her, sliding in and out, veins popping everywhere. Sensations ran through my body like ecstasy as I watched her butt compress and decompress as I picked up my pace again.

Smack! Smack! Smack! I was almost there again. I lowered myself to lay on top her, hugging her, riding that ass. I grinded on it and she drove it back at me. I rocked that ass. I wiggled on that ass. I did everything I could to that pussy. That pussy beat my ass, as I rocked and rolled like a monkey riding her back. She became my addiction as I kissed her neck and licked around her ears, sucking her earlobes while she threw it on me. I bit her gently as I began to cum again. I drilled her for her oil, but she was getting mine as I burst inside her, humping for all I was worth, until at last, I was worth no more.

I stroked my last stroke and collapsed on top of her. She gyrated her hips a little and I could feel her muscles grip me while I rested inside her warmth. It felt so good. I lay there for a few more minutes before I rolled over, pulling myself out of her. Our sweet funk filled the air. She crawled over to me, kissing me lightly.

"Lesson Three. You're never finished when you're finished. You always hold your woman after you make love to her. Let her know it's about her, not the pussy." she advised me.

"What if we fall asleep? My mom might catch us."

"She's working overtime." She kissed me. "Plus, I have the car remember?" She rolled onto her side and pulled my arm around her. I snuggled up to her, my chest to her back, and went to sleep.

Our escapades continued for her stay. She taught me how to love a woman physically, emotionally, and how to appreciate a woman and to let her know it. But, most of all she taught me how not to fall in love with pussy, for she broke my heart when she left.

Miss Delicious

"Hey Yum Yum." a young woman's teasing voice called.

I kept walking through the school's halls wondering what kind of dude had the name "Yum Yum?" When I got to my locker I found out. A note fell out as soon as I opened it. It was addressed:

To: Yum Yum

From: Miss Delicious

I guess I was the kind of guy with the name "Yum Yum." But who was Miss Delicious?

I looked around for a likely suspect, hoping I'd find one who looked delicious. Instead I found four, huddled up giggling and whispering, looking at me and giggling some more. Their ringleader was fine ass Michelle. I walked over to them.

"What's up?"

"Hey Yum Yum." they chimed in harmony and burst out laughing.

What the hell was all this? "Why ya'll tripping? You know my name ain't 'Yum Yum.'" I probably sounded a little upset in my frustration.

"Chill out boy." their ringleader spoke up. "We're just playing with you."

"So why y'all calling me Yum Yum?"

"Because you like to eat." she said with a devilish, but I must say sexy grin. Her mob started laughing again.

"What are you talking about?" I asked still unaware of their implication.

"You know, how you love to eat. How it's yummy to your tummy.'"

They laughed again. It finally hit me though. I blushed under my brown skin. Keisha and her big mouth. I'd told her she was yummy to my tummy when she'd asked me why I loved her pearl so much. What a joy her loose lips would bring me! I just hadn't known it then. Her friends knew I was loyal to her when we were together. A few had even hinted that they'd like a go at me, but I wouldn't betray Keisha like that. Now that she was gone the vultures were swarming over the carcass of our relationship, except they were waiting for me to feed on them.

I thought to myself and smiled. "So, which one of you is Miss Delicious?'" I asked in the deepest tone I could muster.

Now it was their turn to blush. There was only quietness and fidgeting now. Yeah, they were real bold on the offensive. Their defense was no good though. Except for Michelle's.

"Maybe you'll just have to taste us and find out." she said crossing her arms.

"Michelle!" Renee yelped, giving her a slight push on the shoulder.

"Maybe I will." I told them wiggling my tongue at them for emphasis and turned and walked away. Dang. Keisha hadn't been gone much more than a month and here I was with more potential sex than I knew what to do with.

Since I'd made love to Keisha that first time I'd never laid hands on another woman. Keisha more than satisfied my hunger. We'd made love no less than five or six times a week, usually more on the weekends when we weren't held up by school. During our time I'd grown experienced in pleasing her with my tongue. But, in the end she was still Keisha of the grandma dresses because she'd only do missionary style and wouldn't return my oral favors. Things had become a little dull by the time she moved. Though I'd loved her no less, I'd always hoped she'd open up.

All day it seemed eyes were on me. The eyes of girls in my classes. In the halls. I got so paranoid I thought my teacher Mrs. Ross was looking at my tongue when I spoke up to answer her questions. I was tripping. But, not so much as I thought though. After last period my suspicions were confirmed. At my locker I felt a tap on my shoulder. I turned around expecting to see Roscoe or Duck. This tiny chick was looking up at me.

"Aren't you Lane?" she asked with a bold shyness.

"Yeah. What's up?"

She took my hand and slipped me a piece of paper. "Call me okay?"

"Sure." What the hell, I thought. She wasn't bad looking. After she left I stood at my locker deep in contemplation, eyes unseeing, when I backed up to close it and bumped into Michelle and her three hench women.

She questioned me like she was my lady. "Who was that?"

"I don't know. Some chick."

"What'd she want with you, L?" Gwen asked.

"I don't know. She was just saying Hi." I lied. Something was up. Her friends stood behind her with their hands on their hips looking at me while she and Michelle interrogated me.

"Why y'all pressing me woman?" I asked Gwen.

"Boy, ain't nobody pressing you." Michelle said.

Another girl passed. "Hey Lane." she greeted me.

"What's up?"

What was this, open season since Keisha had left? Gwen glared at the girl.

"Where you going Yum Yum?" Michelle taunted me.

"Home to eat." If they wanted to play games I could play games. Her friends laughed.

"You need a ride?"

"Yeah. I ain't trying to walk." I followed her

and her giggling trio to her car. I opened the front passenger door.

"Where you think you're going?" Michelle asked me over the roof.

"I'm going to sit down."

"Oh no you ain't. You got to sit in the back."

"Why?"

"Because you're getting limo service today." she said with a smile. "You can't ride up front with the chauffer."

I got in the back, sandwiched between Renee and Tasha. Gwen sat up front with Michelle. As we rode off Michelle told me they had to stop by Renee's house first. That was cool with me. I wasn't in a hurry. I didn't say anything, but I did feel a nervous excitement building up in the car. I could sense something was up.

When we got there they all jumped out and ran in the house leaving me in the car to wait. Five minutes went by, then ten. What the hell were they doing? You know a brother can't be left waiting like this. I got out and rang the bell. Renee opened the door and pulled me in. My eyes almost popped out my head. She was wearing a towel that was struggling to cover her healthy breasts, ending its fall right on top of some slim red thighs. She led me to her room.

"Where's Michelle and them?" I asked her at the door.

"Waiting for us." She opened the door.

It was deja-vu times three when I entered.

Michelle, Gwen and Tasha were all in their bras and panties looking fine and thick in the ass as only young sisters can. Jack the Black Vagina Finda, being the soldier that he is, stood at attention. Michelle in all her boldness stepped to me.

"Didn't I tell you we were going to take care of you?"

"Yeah." I said with a dry mouth.

"You ready for your taste test?" She reached out to feel Jack from the confines of his uniform.

The girls came together as a unit kissing my neck and rubbing my chest, butt and body as Michelle loosened my pants to play the part of masseuse to Jack.

"Girl, Keisha wasn't lying when she said he was packing."

She pulled me out as Tasha, short and thick with cocoa skin taunt over the two half basket balls in the back of her panties, pulled off my shirt. Renee, average, slim and tight with full sprouting breasts, assisted Michelle by pulling my pants down to my knees. Gwen, around 5'8", hazel eyes, jet black with the prettiest complexion of deep chocolate, thick lush hair, and the full lips of a goddess of temptation, came at me from behind. I could feel the press of her hardening nipples against my bare back as she embraced me, rubbing my chest and stomach. She kissed the back and sides of my neck. I was in heaven. The touching of my body in all places at once was an unforeseen thrill that turned me on like I hadn't experienced with

Keisha. I was feeling the moment and licked my lips.

"You like that?" Michelle fondled my sack.

Gwen reached down from behind me and pumped Jack in slow mo.

"Yeah."

I leaned over to touch and kiss each of the girl's bodies whenever I could because my movement was restricted by my pants around my knees. I rubbed their firm round butts. I've always been a butt and leg man. A breast man too. Shoot, I'm a body man and each of them possessed a beautiful body. From Michelle, whom I'd yet to feel, with long light brown legs, slim at the bottom, thickening to juicy thighs, and hips that curved to a butt that hugged those hips and wasn't too big or small. It was perfect like the shape of a pear with the soft firmness of youth. Her stomach was flat. Her breasts light brown morsels under slightly browner tips, matching her complexion and red tinted hair. Then Tasha, short and plump, but not fat, with a big ass and thighs that were tight as if she worked out, and a small waistline in comparison to her spreading hips and only a mouthful of firm perky peaks rested upon her chest with little nibbles on the ends for my mouth. All of them were variations of Tasha or Michelle in different heights or shades. I adored each of them.

Using Jack as my leash, Gwen guided me to the floor. They held me steady, because with my pants and boxers around my knees I was unstable.

They laid me on my back. Each took a portion of my body as their own to kiss and feel as I feebly attempted to caress them. Gwen told me to relax as Renee and Tasha held my arms and hands down and began kissing my neck and chest from each side. I relished their lips wishing they would let me kiss them so tenderly. Gwen gave Jack a full body rub down when Michelle stepped over my body with her hands on her hips. Her panties and bra had been removed. I could see her dark triangle of love, bushy and tangled, with pinkness winking at me from her center.

"You ready to find Miss Delicious?" she asked me, running her middle finger down under her navel into her bush to rub herself and to finally hide it within as she squatted over my chest. Her finger reappeared shining before my face as I watched her, impulsively licking my lips. My head raised to meet her finger as she rubbed it on my lips and stuck it in my mouth. I sucked on it. I got harder. Mmmm. She retrieved it from my mouth to put it in her again. I could see her, inches away from my face, playing in her pussy. Rubbing her lips in a circular motion with two fingers and then sticking a finger inside and rubbing her mound with her palm. She stared at me intensely while she worked it. I licked my lips, straining my neck to give her a tongue lashing. That pussy smelled good.

All of a sudden I felt moisture and heat engulfing jack. Oh shit! Not since Miss Wilson had I felt such a gripping and pulling sensation.

It was like the hottest pussy gripping me and teasing me all at once. I looked under Michelle to see Gwen engulfing Jack to the best of her ability. Then she pulled it out, slurping on it and licked underneath, now the sides. She sucked my balls and engulfed him again while Michelle stirred herself up, keeping that hot pussy right in front of me. This was too much. I was about to cum.

"Oh shit! Ooh shit!" I exclaimed as my hips rose to meet Gwen's lips.

Michelle looked back to see what was going on.

"Stop it. He's going to cum too soon." Michelle commanded her.

"No! Don't stop!" I cried. That was the first time in months Jack had been treated like that. Man! I didn't know what I was missing with Keisha.

"Not yet." Michelle instructed.

Not yet? What the hell was she waiting on? I never got the chance to voice my frustration. When I'd laid my head back in ecstasy and closed my eyes, Michelle had positioned herself over my lips. Now she lowered herself to give me a taste test. Her strong thighs held her steady while she squatted, hands on her knees. She worked my lips, doing the "Do-Do Brown" dance on my lips and nose. I opened my mouth to receive her but her motions required nothing of me but to stick my tongue out as she rode my nose, chin, lips or whatever. She indiscriminately plastered herself all over my face. I tried to grab her and show her what I could really do, but Renee and Tasha kept my arms pinned down. I guess they didn't know I was trying to free my arms so I could position her just right and take care of business. They thought I was trying to buck. They held me firmly as Gwen played with Jack and fondled my balls while sitting on my legs.

"Ahh, ummm." Michelle moaned as she worked her bush on my face. Her rose petals were rubbing their dew on my lips for me to test. I wanted to reach up and squeeze her butt. I wanted to squeeze it as I moved it to where I could properly get at that pussy. I could only stick my tongue out as far as I could to tickle her tender parts. It seemed she was getting off on my nose which she had found was convenient for her to ride to her peak on its peak. She was cumming and cumming and I could smell her getting hotter and wetter and muskier as she came. She moaned and grunted grinding in a mad fury on my face until at last she came to a halt. I was so happy. I was tired of this foolishness. They didn't know what the hell they were doing. When Michelle rolled over in her exhaustion and the girls eased up their hold on me so Gwen could take her place on the saddle of my face I used all my strength to twist and turn and freed myself. I shook them off.

"Get the fuck off me!" I roared standing up.

They cowered now, thinking I was angry at the rape of my tongue and face.

"Y'all don't know what the fuck you're doing." They looked at me in fear as I stepped out of my pants and boxers completely. "You want your pussy ate, huh? Huh!" I looked at each one of them. "You think you're Miss Delicious?" My body was trembling, all six feet and two inches of me. Just like Jack and all eight inches of him. "We're going to find out if I'm Mr. Delicious and all of you are Yum Yums. Come here Michelle." I commanded. She looked at me nervously with wide innocent looking eyes. Lying ass eyes. "I said come here." I told her firmly.

She stepped forward slowly. I grabbed her hand and jerked her to me and kissed her full on the mouth.

"You like that taste, huh?"

She looked down and said nothing. Her friends were shuffling around looking embarrassed for her. Oh, the fun had just started. I pushed her down. She resisted.

"Oh, you ain't so bold now are you? You act like you don't know what to do." I pushed her out of the way. "Gwen." I called looking at her motioning with my head. "Show her how it's done."

I lay back on the floor with Jack still standing at attention. Gwen got on her hands and knees, crawled between my legs, and took my throbbing muscle in her mouth. She put her lips over my tip and ran her tongue in circles before she deep throated his length. I grunted my pleasure. I felt weak again, like she was sucking my energy. My head fell back. Up and down she went with the long slow and then fast strokes of a pro. I opened my eyes. Renee stood there with her thighs so slim and contoured perfectly.

"Come here." I instructed her. She came to me and looked down. "Let me see what that stuff tastes like."

She stepped out of her panties, stepped over my head and squatted down. I placed my palms on the bottom of her butt and thighs to position her while I spread her moist lips with my thumbs. She looked so soft and delicate like a rose with petals fresh from a new blossoming. I readied myself to taste her, but Gwen had sped up. She was into it like she loved my girth stretching her jaws. I looked under Renee to see her head bobbing in a rhythm.

"Not so fast. Slow down." I told her so I wouldn't come too quickly.

After she eased up I lowered Renee to my waiting tickler and using the tip of my tongue licked the inside of each of her lips, one by one. I felt her body quiver enjoying my touch. She smelled good too. I stuck my tongue deep in her slit and curled it upwards. She inhaled deeply with a hiss. Her body jerked.

"You like that?" I asked her.

"Um hum."

I opened wide, flattened my tongue, and put my mouth on her pussy and wiggled it, pressed it, and slid it in her using her lips as guides. I kissed it with light feathery kisses.

"Umm um. This pussy tastes good. You think you're Miss Delicious?"

"Um hum." she said, dropping more of her weight to my hands and her pussy on my face.

"Rub that thang on me so I can get a good taste."

She rocked in slow movements to the rhythm of my tongue massaging her insides until I felt her legs weaken. If I was standing mine would have been weak too. Gwen was taking Jack out of her mouth and licking the bottom of my shaft and nuts with tenderness. I was about to cum. I raised my knees to move her off me. My plans were not ready for that yet. I put my lips around Renee's engorged clit and sucked on it. I fiddled with it and sucked on it, stroking it with my tongue, until she came. I lapped up her juices as her knees gave out, dropping her on my face, weak, trembling and panting like a thoroughbred after the Kentucky Derby.

"Mmmm mmm. That's some good pussy." I was feeling this now and was in my mode. I pushed Renee off me and looked around. "Come here Gwen. Tasha, you know what to do." I watched Renee crawl to the side and lay down while Michelle just stood there looking crazy as I served her friends.

Tasha came between my legs gripping my staff as Gwen took her position over my head. She was dripping wet already when she started to lower herself to my shining lips. I held her right above my mouth letting her juice drop on my waiting tongue. I tasted it, smacking my lips.

"Damn girl, you might just be Miss Delicious. You think you're the one?"

"You taste it for yourself." she sassed me.

"Oh, you think you're like that?"

"Try it and see."

Tasha was lathering me up sloppily as I lowered Gwen to my expectant jaws of life. That stuff was so hot I almost burned my lips. I let my tongue give her one slow pressing and probing thrust. This girl was ridiculous! That thang was fat, wet, hot, and intoxicating. Her scent was more than intoxicating. This chick was Marisol all over! I pushed her off me and yelled next.

"Un unh boy. I know you ain't doing me like that." she spit out.

"Chill it ain't over. Move Tasha." She wasn't doing much anyway. I looked around. I didn't want anymore head. It was good but nothing like the inside of a woman. "Come get on this dick Renee."

As she came I looked over at Michelle standing there naked, fine as hell, chewing her fingernails rubbing her legs together. Serves her right. Trying to abuse a brother's face.

Renee squatted over Jack. He eagerly jumped and swayed, waiting to be enveloped inside her. She took him with one hand, spread herself with the other, and eased him into her juice soaked pussy. Oh she was tight and hot. I could feel her walls stretching to accommodate my girth. She bit her lower lip, closed her eyes, and eased herself down on me. She went slow to take all she could. She slid up and down on it until she had it lubricated with her juices dropped on it and paused before she began her ride. Tasha stepped up, ready to take her place. I looked under her to see Renee's slim thighs raise her up and lower her again with her hands supporting her on my stomach. I could see Jack glistening playing hide and seek within her tight confines. I told Tasha to turn around so I could see that big ass and all that pussy from the back as she came to me. When she was coming down to take her place her cheeks spread to reveal a neatly trimmed mound with pink cotton candy puckering lips puckering up to kiss me. I spread her cheeks a little more and French kissed her candy lips. She pushed back against my tongue. I broke the kiss.

"You see that dick sliding in and out that pussy?" I asked her. "You want my tongue in you like that?"

"Yes." she answered me.

"Tell me you want to feel my tongue inside you."

"L, I want to feel your tongue in me." she said backing her lovely curves up.

I kissed her cheeks, licking the cuff at the bottom. I kissed the bottom of her lips down to the top to flick her clit with my tongue. She tensed and tightened her muscles trapping my nose deeply buried between her cheeks. I rubbed my tongue between her lips, pulled them apart with my thumbs and stuck it in her channel as deep as I could and whirled it around. I sucked on her getting more into it as I felt Renee riding me with a passion. I thrust my hips up to meet her pulsing hotness. I spread Tasha's lips again and slid a finger in her.

"You like that?" I asked her.

She didn't say anything, she just backed up to impale herself on my finger. I stuck another in her, curving them down to meet my thumb on the outside rubbing her clit. She moaned, rocking with the motion of my fingers. I craned my neck up, boring my face between her hills and licked a sloppy wet circle around her tight butt. She jerked forward.

"Oh shit!" she exclaimed.

"You like that Miss Delicious booty?"

She must have, because she rocked back to let me do it again. Again I rimmed her and stuck my tongue in the middle while I worked my fingers in her, loosening her up. Renee was pounding herself on me. She'd leaned back on her hands with her elbows locked and was cumming again. I was cumming too and moved quickly to the side to pull myself out of her.

"Damn Lane, Shit!" she caught her breath looking at me in a frustrated manner.

I sucked on Tasha's waiting slit again, feeling Jack jump and jerk leaking. I pulled on it a few time to drain everything out before putting my fingers in Tasha only to retrieve them so I could suck them.

"Now that's some delicious pussy and ass." I joked.

I was on top of the world. I pushed Tasha down so she could take her place on my rod, still jumping and wet with Renee's cum. She took it in her hand and eased it in her. I fit easily. Though not as tight as Renee, she was hotter and had some mean body action that had me brimming again. I grabbed her hips and worked with her.

"Slow down a little bit." I told her.

Gwen came and stood over me looking down at me expectantly. "What're you doing?" I demanded of her.

"Lane, I know you ain't going to leave me hanging like that."

I ignored her, concentrating on working Tasha as she sped up working herself up to a frenzy riding me. She "Ooohed and aahed." and moaned while she worked that pussy until it started sucking and popping. Her musk permeated the air putting a new drive in me. I gripped her a little more firmly and rose up to meet her downward slide on my pole.

"Oooh shit girl you good."

She looked in my eyes as she dropped down on me again. I could feel myself brimming again as she bottomed out and ground her box on me.

"You like this pussy L?"

"Yeah baby. That pussy's good."

Tired of standing around, Gwen tried to squat on my face. I closed my mouth and shook my head. She dropped on me and closed her thighs around my face. Her scent was right in my nose.

Her hair was brushing my chin.

"You gonna eat this pussy boy!"

Damn this woman was just like Marisol! I loved it. I pushed Tasha off me. Jack left her with a slight sucking sound, our smell igniting the room. I grabbed Gwen by her arms and rolled her over on her back. She kept her thighs firmly locked on me.

"Let me go," I told her. "and I'll show you why they call me Yum Yum for real. Come on. Let me go."

"Don't be playing with me Lawrence."

"I ain't playing, let me go. I'll do it."

She released my head. I stood up over her. She lay there on her back with her legs spread wide in anticipation of getting ate. That sexy you know what. I was on her so bad I was damn near scared to get it.

"Wait a minute. Let me catch my breath." I looked for another excuse to prolong it. I saw Michelle still standing there with her chest heaving like she was having an asthma attack. "Get over here Michelle." I ordered her.

She almost jumped to me. After being left out so long she'd become anxious, rubbing her thighs together like she was starting a fire between her legs. Seems like it was working too, because a trickle of her natural lubrication was leaking down her pretty brown thighs. I put a hand behind her head, pulled her to me and gave her pussy a wet kiss. She responded eagerly. Her tongue desperately entered my mouth to search for mine. I felt between her legs for her bush and slipped a finger in her. Her knees quivered. I broke our kiss, looked at her, and stuck the finger in her mouth. She sucked it greedily. Taking her by the hand I pulled her down with me between Gwen's spread thighs to her waiting sex.

I spread Gwen's lips and licked her, tracing my tongue from the top down to her center. I kissed and sucked her. Her hands rubbed my head. I licked her core, jabbing my tongue inside. I came up for air and kissed Michelle. She tried to suck my tongue out my mouth. I broke away and pushed her between Gwen's legs. There was no resistance. She kissed around Gwen's thighs, licking a teasing circle around Gwen's hot spot. I moved behind Michelle's uplifted butt. That fat wet pussy looked at me, just dripping wet. I rubbed Jack on top of her ass, up and down her crack, sliding it between her lips and back up. Gwen moaned as Michelle sucked her up. Michelle seemed to be releasing all the excitement she'd built up watching me suck and fuck her friends on Gwen. She had two fingers inside her pushing them in and out. Gwen grabbed a handful of Michelle's hair and thrust her hips at her as they moaned their lust to each other. Michelle pulled her fingers out and sucked them only to start licking around Gwen's clit. She stuck the fingers back in her. I stopped rubbing my wood on Michelle's slit and entered her. She moaned, licking Gwen as she took what I had to give. I gripped her cheeks with my palms flat and spread her so I could watch me slide in and out of her lips. I drove in and out of her, building up a shining sheen as I pounded my eight inches into her core.

"Umm umm umm umm." Michelle moaned into Gwen's pussy each time I rocked her.

"Oh. Oh. Ssss. Ummmn." Gwen let loose as Michelle put her pleasure from me into her tongue action for Gwen.

I felt my tide rising again. I hit it harder, gripping that ass, banging it into my groin.

"Ungh ungh ungh." Michelle grunted as I mashed into her.

I could feel her walls pulsing as I beat that pussy. She came, heating my pole even more as she creamed on me. With my excitement building I pounded myself in and out of those lush lips. Gwen drove Michelle's face into her cunt as her hips lifted off the floor to meet her lips and tongue. I could hear her pants of pleasure betraying her cumming from getting her pussy ate by another woman. Her moans and groan were loudly muffled. I pulled out of Michelle and went forward to Gwen. She took a hand off Michelle's head and took me into her mouth. She sucked me hungrily as I came, swallowing and gulping my cum. She sucked on me as if she could drain my essence through my penis to empower her. It seemed to be working. Her head bobbing, she grabbed my nuts. I could see her cheeks caving in and filling out as I released my load in her mouth. She greedily swallowed every drop as I sank down on my back. Moving from under Michelle's lips she pulled a semi-hard Jack out of her mouth and climbed astride me. Maneuvering herself over me she eased Jack inside her engorged cunt, swollen from the beating it had taken from Michelle's tongue. I slid in her and felt the heart of fire. Like a coat on a winter's day the warmth revived Jack and, being the soldier that he is, he came to attention. I could only lie there panting for air, trying to catch my breath. Renee took advantage of my weakened state and mounted my lips again facing Gwen. I savored Gwen's hotness while enjoying my second helping of Renee. Gwen proved the old saying true. Her blackberry was far sweeter than anything I'd ever experienced. She worked that thing on me as if she was trying to convince me that she was the baddest out of me and her, that she'd teach me a lesson. She did. Her pussy was too good, too hot, too right. I tried not to think about how I was feeling. I looked around me, trying to distract myself before Gwen made me cum again. Tasha was taking advantage of Michelle's exhaustion. She rolled her over and straddled her face. Michelle, her lessons well learned, licked Tasha to the point of ecstasy. I watched the show, turned on by their lust. It pushed me to my point again. I pushed Gwen off and stirred Renee with my tongue. She took her cue and leaned over, putting us in a 69, and deep throated my pussy wet meat. I sucked her as I came and she sucked me, our bodies lunging for the other's expectant lips. When it was all over we laid out on the floor, naked, sweaty, and smelling of pussy. Gwen spoke up from where she lay resting her head on her hands.

"So Yum Yum, which of us is Miss Delicious?"

I grinned. "I don't know. You all taste so good it's a tie. I think we'll have to break the tie tomorrow." Oh, I knew who it was that had that get-back, but I'd never tell her that. She'd have me wide open and wrapped around her finger.

They agreed. "We'll be waiting for you after school." they said in unison.

It was great being **Yum Yum**.

145

I headed northbound on interstate 85 looking for some more whores that could put their whore-ish escapades down on paper or at least maybe I could get fucked by some freaks who could act out what they wish they could write. I got my dick sucked in North Carolina a couple of times but nothin' special happened. I fucked a midget in Virginia who swore up and down that she wasn't a midget, she kept saying that she was just short. She had one of those compacted midget fat asses so I got a good buzz off of some Vodka and orange juice and some good Cali weed I don't leave home without and fucked this lil bitch for about two days, well, not really two days but at least twenty minutes. You could say I kinda cut it short, pun intended. I ended up in Tennessee, lookin' to bag this one girl who obviously had some serious talent because her name was ringin' when it came to short erotic stories. Any story the last girl would've wrote would've been a short story, lol... but anyway. This Tennessee girl was the bizness, I could tell and hadn't even met her yet. I thought aight well I'ma get some ass from a freak with skills, but when I met her I came to find out that she was happily married with children and seemed more of the Zane type who thought and wrote smut but didn't act it out.

Seeing that Zane is the best that ever did it, I gained control of my libido and professionally checked her out. The girl had innumerable sex stories and she was really driven. I liked her so much I'ma let you see for yourself. She calls herself Envy. It fits the emotion other female writers may have for her. Her story is called Straight fuckin'.

Straight Fucking
By Envy
©2017

"Oh Baby!" Wayne moaned as I slurped on his big dick.

When I rolled my tongue around his dickhead, I felt his stomach cave in. I looked down at his feet. His toes were curled. I was a bonafide freak and I was doing my job. I believed in pleasing my man because I damn sure didn't want him going elsewhere.

"Oh, Trina, I'm about to cum!" In less than five minutes my man had came all in my mouth. I opened my mouth and I showed him his babies before swallowing them.

"Mmmm, delicious." I said.

Both tired and sated with sweat, we fell into a deep sleep. A few hours later I felt

Wayne nudge me. I wiped the sleep from my eyes and gave him my undivided attention.

"What is it Baby?" I asked in between a yawn.

"My mama wants us to go to her church revival."

I knew Wayne 's mother didn't care for me so I decided to go to her little church function. This would be the perfect opportunity to win a few brownie points with her.

Nonchalantly, I asked, "When is it?"

"Friday." Wayne said, before climbing out of our huge king-sized bed.

I rolled back over to get a little more sleep before it was time for me to get up.

Morning came all too soon and reluctantly I threw back my Italian sheets and climbed out of bed. After a nice, warm shower

I dressed in a form-fitting black Gucci halter mini-dress. After pinning my long, streaked hair up into a neat bun, I applied a little makeup and slipped my small feet in a pair of black stilettos. I smiled at my reflection, I knew I was the shit. My measurements were 36-24-40, and I was the shit. Couldn't nobody tell me differently.

I grabbed my black Gucci bag and quickly sprinted out the door and jumped into in my black 745.

As I drove down I-65, I felt on top of the world. Wayne was the man of my dreams, but he was afraid of commitment. I knew I was wrong for cheating on him, but a lot of shit had happened to me when I was a little girl, bad shit. My mother was a crack addict who was always looking for her next big hit. When I was thirteen she used to sell me for crack. As

I got older I found out that I was a beautiful girl, but everything that had happened to me had brought my self esteem all the way down and know this.

I really love Wayne, but I use men for all I can get out of them because that's what my mother did my entire childhood.

I turned down Hillshire Drive and made my way to Jordan Lyon's house. As I parked on the street in front of his house, I made sure his wife's blue Volvo wasn't there.

I picked up my Blackberry and called Jordan.

"Hi Sweetie!" he said.

Instantly, I began to blush. Jordan was a wealthy business man who gave me everything my heart desired. Any time I needed something I called him. He was my "Sugar

Daddy." Although he was twenty-five years older than me, his dick was the bomb.

"Where are you?" he asked huskily.

"In front of your house."

"Well come on in." He said.

Excitedly, I jumped out of the car and made my way up his long walkway. Since the door was already unlocked I let myself in. I opened the door and called out to him. Jordan appeared out of nowhere. He grabbed my hand and led me to the bedroom.

"Wait, you not going to show me around?" I asked, looking around his home in awe.

Although we'd been straight fucking for several months, this was the first time we'd ever met at his house.

"Baby, I think we should go ahead and fuck so you can leave. Honestly, I don't know when my wife will be back." he said nervously.

"Nonsense." I said, placing my Gucci bag down on the leather couch. "It won't take long. I want a grand tour." I whined.

"Okay," he said.

It took me twenty minutes to see the house in its entirety. Everything looked amazing and I couldn't believe people actually lived like this. Jordan even had a movie theater and a recreation room. Even though he footed the bill for my penthouse monthly, I wanted more. I needed more.

"Are you ready Baby?" he asked sensuously.

I nodded my head and he led me to the bedroom. I pushed him down onto the bed and danced seductively in front of him. When he licked his lips, I knew he wanted me but I didn't want to rush our morning. This was our moment and I had to put it on him if I wanted him to take me on a shopping spree. He reached out to me but I took a few steps back.

"Uh uh, I'm about to strip for you."

No sooner than I had taken off my shirtdress we heard some keys.

"Oh, shit! Maria is back!" Jordan said as he picked up my mini-dress and stuck me in the closet.

"What the hell are you doing?" I asked hotly.

"Please, just go along with me." he said pleadingly with puppy dog eyes.

I conceded, got into the closet and he closed the door on me. The closet door was cracked just a little so that I could see his old ass wife walk in. Although she was holding a little extra weight around the midsection, she looked really good for her age. Maria stood about five feet six inches tall and her butterscotch skin was flawless. Her long black, wavy hair hung to the middle of her back.

"Hi Love." She purred, as she walked over to him. "Who's car is that parked in front of our house?" she asked inquisitively.

He stood from the bed and walked over to the window. Looking out, he hunched his shoulders.

"I don't know." he lied. "Someone probably had car trouble."

She dropped the subject and walked over to him, kissing him softly on the neck. I know they weren't about to make love right in front of me. She pulled off her blue blouse. Jordan took one of her nipples in his mouth. As he sucked her nipple her head fell back and she moaned. After laying her across the bed he pulled off his clothes. After practically ripping off her skirt, he dropped down to his knees and began eating her out. Maria was moaning like crazy.

"Does this feel good to you Baby?" he asked huskily.

"Oh yes." she moaned. He ate her out for another twenty minutes before he stood up and laid across the bed. Now it was Maria's turn to pleasure him. For an older lady she sure knew how to suck a mean dick. If Jordan's moaning was any indication, she was doing one helluva job and it kinda made me jealous. I wanted to be the one to please him like that. Switching positions several times, they really seemed like they were enjoying themselves. Suddenly, I wondered what in the hell I was doing there. Seemed liked Jordan's home was one happy one. Maria climbed on top of her husband and straddled his thighs. Slowly, she came down on his dick and rode him like someone half her age. I couldn't deny it, this bitch had mad skills.

"Oh Maria." he moaned. I was getting sick at the stomach.

"Yes." she said through clenched teeth. "Fuck me Daddy."

Maria rode our man into ecstasy and after climbing off, she retreated to the bathroom. Once the shower water started he rushed over to the closet and said, "You have to go before she comes out."

I said, "Surely, you are going to give me some money for my trouble of coming all the way over her and not getting anything."

Quickly, he ran back over to the bed and snatched his pants from the floor. He reached into his pocket and pulled out a wad of twenties. After grabbing my Gucci bag from the leather couch he walked me to the door, kissed me on my cheek and promised to call me later on that week. Once I got into my car, I counted the money and realized I had more than a thousand dollars. Boy, Jordan sure knew how to take care of me. I would thank him later.

I started the engine and I quickly drove off. I had to find someone to put out the fire that Jordan had started. My pussy was dripping and I was ready to fuck. I thought over my possibilities and knew I couldn't get Wayne. He was at work. I sighed and called Jonathan. He answered on the third ring.

"Hi." I purred.

"Who is this?"

"Uh Katrina." I said.

I was greeted by complete silence. For a minute I thought he'd hung up. Jonathan was my last boyfriend and when I met Wayne I broke up with him. He was still bitter but I just wanted some dick so I didn't give a fuck about his feelings.

"Jon, are you there?"

"Yeah, what do you want?"

"Er, I was wondering if you wanted company."

Just as I expected, he didn't deny me and I was on my way to my ex lover's house. The twenty minute drive was well worth it, because I was anticipating feeling his eight inch dick deep inside me. Stepping to the door, I didn't even have to knock. The door came open and I stepped into the cool house. Jonathan took my hand and led me to his bedroom. Sitting on his bed, we tried to watch a little BET but his hands started to roam and I knew it was on from there.

"Take your clothes off," he ordered.

I did as I was told. Jonathan's voice always made my libido act in a way I couldn't quite understand. It was if he had some kind of power over me. As I undressed he watched. His eyes never left my body. As he licked his lips, my pussy began to drip. Jonathan's body was still as fine as ever. Licking my lips, I couldn't wait to fuck this man. As I began to drop to my knees, he stopped me.

"Wait, I want to taste you first."

Jonathan's head was buried deep between my thighs as he feasted on my womanhood. As he slurped on my juices, he took my pink bud in his mouth and my head fell back. I was on the verge of an orgasm when he stopped.

"Why the hell did you stop?" I asked.

"Trina, I want to talk to you."

"About?" I asked, the attitude evident in my voice. I wanted him to eat my pussy and then fuck the shit out of me so I could go. Wayne would be home in about an hour and a half.

"I've missed you and I wanted to get back with you."

"Jon, you know I have a boyfriend. I can't leave him for you."

"Why not? You left me for him."

He had a point but I felt a connection with Wayne that I'd been missing with Jonathan. We'd been together for more than two years but when I met Wayne I was blown away by his swagger and confidence. It wasn't long before he had my nose wide open. Within the first six months of talking to Wayne , I left

Jonathan. And although he was heartbroken, I didn't give a damn.

"No!" I said firmly.

Jonathan stood from the bed and began getting dressed. I watched him in amazement. I knew damn well he wasn't going to leave me here, horny as hell.

"You got to go." he said, pointing to the door.

I closed my legs, snatched up my thong and mini-dress and sauntered to his bathroom. After I got dressed I didn't even look at Jonathan. I stormed out of the house and slammed the door. When I pulled off from his house I burned rubber. My next stop was Marvel. He was the definition of thug lovin'. For some reason he always knew how to make me get extra freaky, fucking in the ass and everything. Pulling up to Marvel's condo I parked and looked around. He didn't live in the best area but for him I'd make much sacrifice. Killing the engine, I climbed out the car and made my way up to door number 302B. One knock and Marvel instantly opened the door. It was as if he was waiting just for me. I walked through the door and he immediately jumped all over me. We didn't make it to the bedroom, we fucked right there on the living room floor like beasts. Marvel stripped off all my clothing and dropped to his knees, feasting on my yum yum. My head fell back moaning as he ate me.

He asked me, "Who's pussy is this?"

There was no thinking about that question.

At the present moment's it was Marvel's and I quickly answered his question.

Suddenly he stopped.

"I want to try something different. Lay down on your stomach and spread your legs."

I did as I was told and soon I heard the distinct sound of a vibrator. After lubricating the vibrator, he stood the seven inch dildo in my ass. After I relaxed a bit, the feeling started to drive me wild. As he fucked my ass with the dildo I ran my fingers over my sensitive pink bud. Within minutes I came all over the floor. Replacing the vibrator with his dick, Marvel fucked my ass, nice and slow. As he stroked my ass I called out his name. This man was an incredible lover and if I didn't love Wayne so much I'd leave him. Marvel just wasn't the settling down type and I didn't want to rush him into something he really didn't want. After about ten minutes of fucking me in the ass, he wiped his dick off with a wet wipe he had nearby then he slipped his hard shaft into my pussy from the back. His breathing became staggered and so did mine as I grinded my hips to his thrusts. Pulling his dick out, he came all over my bubbly ass. I wasn't ready to leave yet, so I took his engorged manhood in my mouth and slurped and salivated all over it. I was driving him crazy from my dick sucking skills and I was more than happy I was pleasing him. After deep throating him a few times he came again. I hated to fuck and leave but I did have a man to get to. Gathering my things I went to his bathroom and took a wash up. After throwing on my clothes I left and all the way home I smiled from the throbbing sensation between my legs. The day hadn't been such a waste after all. I was a pure nymphomaniac and I needed dick like a crack head needed their next rock.

When Wayne stepped through the door I was standing there in nothing but my birthday suit. His mouth fell open as he made his way over to me. Instantly, my pussy began to throb. I was ready to feel Wayne's nine inch dick. I led him to the bathroom. While he showered, I lit candles and put on some R. Kelly.

After ten minutes Wayne emerged from the bathroom, butt naked. He had a body like a NFL player and I loved every inch of his six foot frame. He walking over to me and pushed me back on the bed. He started at my toes and suckled each one. He then made his way up to my pussy. When he stuck his hot tongue in my pussy, I squirmed from the pleasure.

"Be still!" he ordered, before he grabbed my wide hips.

He held me in place and he ate my pussy for more than twenty minutes. After I came all in his mouth, he positioned himself on top of me and buried his dick deep inside of me.

I arched my back and allowed him entry to my treasure chest. As his thrusts became powerful, I called out his name and met his thrust by moving my hips to his rhythm. In that moment I'd made up my mind. I wasn't going to cheat on my man anymore. He gave me all that I needed. My head fell back from sheer pleasure as Wayne fucked me like never before.

"Turn around." he ordered.

Quickly, I flipped over onto my stomach. Wayne buried himself deep inside of my wet pussy and drilled the hell out of me. As I worked my hips and threw that pussy back at him, I heard him moan. It gave me great satisfaction when I knew I was pleasing my man. In less than ten minutes he came all inside me. He kissed my neck, stood up and walked into the bathroom. I fixed the sheets and slipped under the covers. In minutes I slipped into a peaceful sleep.

A half an hour later I nervously got dressed for Wayne's mother's church function. Already I'd changed outfits three times. His mother despised me and one day I wanted to be Mrs. Wallace so I knew I had to make her like me.

Wayne appeared behind me, kissed me on the neck and said, "Baby, you look good. Don't change anymore."

Wayne looked handsome as hell in a pair of khaki pants and a light blue collar shirt. It always amazed me how good he looked. His long dreads were neatly pulled back in a ponytail.

I combed through my long streaked hair, I slid my feet in a pair of brown Jimmy Choo pumps. I ran my hands over my brown wrap dress. I sighed, grabbed my purse and bible. Here goes nothing, I thought to myself as I made my way to the living room. After locking up, Wayne and I walked out to his blue Cadillac Escalade. He opened the passenger side door for me and I climbed in.

He slid behind the wheel of the truck, we put on our seat belts and Wayne pulled off. I couldn't lie I was nervous as hell as we made our way to Brown Baptist Church. When we pulled up to the church I was awed by all the people that were there. Bile rose in my throat. I guess Wayne could see the uncomfortable look on my face.

"Baby, don't worry, you're going to be fine." He said to me.

I gave him an uneasy smile as he made his way over to my side. He opened the door for me and I jumped out. Immediately he grabbed my hand and we walked through the doors of the church, hand in hand.

Mrs. Wallace smiled from ear to ear when she saw her son. She rolled her eyes at me and I took a deep breath. As she made her way over to us, I felt out of place and uncomfortable. I had to remember I was there with my man and he wouldn't let his mother disrespect me, no matter what.

"Hi Baby." she said happily to Wayne before placing a kiss on his cheek. She looked over at me and said, "Trina." curtly. Mrs. Wallace wore a tight smile and I knew her feelings for me hadn't changed.

"Hello Mrs. Wallace." I said pleasantly. She was going to make it hard to be her friend. Mrs. Wallace led us to an empty pew and left. I leaned over and whispered into Wayne's ear, "Your mother hates me."

"She loves me and she doesn't want me with anybody. You know how mothers are with their sons. Just give her time Trina."

Halfway through the revival my pussy began to throb. I knew it was wrong to be feeling that way in church, but I needed my man.

Once again I leaned over. I said, "Wayne, I want you."

Wayne didn't ask any questions. We got up and went into a little side room. Everything was decorated beautifully. The pastel colored walls were adorned with a couple pictures. One of Jesus and his disciples and the other of Him parting the red sea. The plush white carpet was extremely thick and comfortable and almost as soon as I stepped in the room I kicked off my three inch stilettos. My small feet sunk in the carpet as I made my way around the room. In the corner of the room sat a huge black entertainment center. The fifty-two inch HDTV wasn't on. Luckily, there was a cherry wood desk in the room. He sat me on the desk, pulled my thong off then propped my legs up. He dropped to his knees and stuck his tongue in my wet and warm pussy.

"Oh!" I moaned, biting my lip.

I knew I had to be quiet. We were in a church of all places. Wayne was pretty horny too, because he practically ripped my dress off. After he removed my black lace bra, he suckled on my left nipple and played with the right one.

"Oh Wayne!" I called out.

We were in our own world and weren't worried about getting caught. I guess that was part of the excitement. Wayne's thrust became more powerful and I whimpered in pleasure.

"Trina, this pussy is too good." he said, as I grinded my hips to his rhythm.

With one swift movement, he picked me up from the desk and placed me on the wall without even breaking his stride from fucking me. As his thick dick pumped in and out of me, my eyes rolled to the back of my head.

We accidentally knocked over a coat rack. Thinking we were safe, we continued. Besides, the music was so loud in the sanctuary I doubted if anybody heard the loud thud from the coat rack. We continued fucking and going at it like two dogs in heat. We switched positions several times before I looked up in

Deacon Kelly's face. I gasped so hard I almost swallowed my tongue. Wayne didn't miss a beat; he continued to beat the pussy up.

I tapped him a little and then whispered, "Look."

Wayne turned around, smiled at Deacon Kelly and said, "Aw, I thought you'd never come."

This time, he pulled his dick out of me and went over to give the older man some dap. Deacon Kelly was well in his fifties. His salt and pepper colored hair was cut into a low fade. His was medium build and short in height. To be an older man, Deacon Kelly wasn't that bad on the eyes.

They both looked at me, grinning like they'd hit the lotto.

"Trina, come to me." Wayne ordered.

I'd do anything for Wayne but this was pushing it. Giving him an incredulous look, I sucked my teeth and put my hands on my hips.

"Bitch, did you hear me?" he asked aggressively.

"Look, I don't think I'm down for this," I said, with much attitude.

"If you don't bring yo ass here you're going to be sorry."

My legs felt heavy as lead as I made my way over to my man.

"I want you to suck my man's dick." he said, pointing at the deacon.

With wide eyes, I stared at my man. Did he really mean the shit he was saying? Not wanting to question him, I dropped to my knees and took the deacon's somewhat erect dick in my mouth. Shockingly, he got hard as soon as I put my mouth on him. He was an impressive seven inches long.

Deacon Kelly rubbed his hands through my long, flowing curls as I slurped on his dick.

"Don't stop! This shit feels so good." The deacon said.

I peeped up a little and saw Wayne sitting over in a leather chair watching. He was still naked so obviously they were about to run a train on me.

After another ten minutes of sucking his dick, the deacon pulled me to my feet and placed me back on the desk.

He looked over his shoulder and he said, "Let's do her like we did Desiree back in the day."

Wayne nodded, stood and walked over to me.

"Stand up." he said.

Once I was standing, Wayne got behind me and stuck his huge dick into my booty hole. Deacon Kelly slid into my wet pussy. Both of them were drilling me at the same time. I almost forgot where the hell I was. My cries of pleasure grew loud but neither seemed to care.

Suddenly, we all heard, "What the fuck???!!!"

All three of us turned to the door to face Deacon Kelly's wife.

"B-B-Baby, I-I can explain. I promise this is not wh-wh-what it looks like." he stammered.

He was standing there with his pants around his ankles. What could he possibly say to get out of this one?

"Do you know how it feels to be talked about? People whisper everywhere I go, about how lowdown my husband is. I didn't want to believe them. I couldn't!" she said, shaking her head fiercely.

I could tell Sister Liz was hurt. A pained expression covered her face. Tears of hurt, pain and confusion streamed down her face.

"I don't want to hear any more of your lies!" she yelled at Deacon Kelly.

Sister Liz pulled out a small handgun from her purse and before anyone could say anything she fired eight shots. I'm sure the other church members heard the long gunshots because Deacon Jones rushed through the door.

"Oh Lord!" he shouted falling to his knees.

Sister Liz was still held the gun in her hand, sobbing like a baby. She's fallen back onto the couch in the corner.

"Sister Liz, what have you done?"

179

Deacon Jones could tell that her nerves were shot. She rocked back and forth, as if looking for comfort.

From a distance, the sound of sirens could be heard.

When the police came through the door they immediately arrested Sister Liz, while several EMTs began working on me, Wayne and Deacon Kelly. Rushed to the hospital, I was immediately taken into surgery. The bullet had pierced a main artery in my arm. At that time, I was unsure of Wayne's condition. After a grueling four hour surgery I was taken to recovery where I worried the hell out of the nurses with questions about Wayne. Each of them gave me a sympathetic grin.

"Honey, right now you should worry about your own recovery." Nurse Jean said.

Unfortunately she walked off before I could ask her anything else. It seemed like they were hiding something from me. After a few hours in recovery I was taken into a hospital room where my mother rushed to be by my side. Looking over at her, I smiled. I wondered if she knew the details of the situation. I hoped not, she'd probably consider me a slut.

"Ma, how's Wayne?" I asked desperately.

I guess she could see the pain in my eyes. Sighing, she stepped closer to my bedside and stroked my arm.

"Baby, I'm sorry to tell you this, but Wayne's on life support. They're not expecting him to make it."

"Nooooo," I screamed. The pain was so real, my body trembled from the ache in my heart. How would I live without him? Wayne and I had plans in life and now they'd all been

181

taken away from us. If I ever got my hands on Sister Liz I was going to kill her. Even though I knew she was a woman scorned, why did she have to take my future?

The recovery process was long and slow. It had been three months and I still hadn't gained much use in my left arm. The doctor's assured me that I'd be one hundred percent again but what about the hole in my heart?

When thinking about that fateful day, it still sends chills down my spine.

It turned out that that wasn't Wayne and Deacon Kelly's first time doing something like that. There had been a big scandal at Brown's Baptist church back in the day when a young woman claimed that the deacon and Wayne had fucked her during church service. It was never proven, but Sister Liz had caught her husband cheating before and that was the last straw. She shot Deacon Kelly in the head, killing him instantly. My poor Wayne wasn't as fortunate. She shot him several times but he didn't die instantly. Wayne fought for his life for seven days before dying. Sister Liz was convicted of two counts of murder and one count of attempted murder. She is currently serving a life sentence.

I Learned from that situation but quiet is kept, I'm still

STRAIGHT FUCKING!

This next cat needs no intro, no back story! His writin' is edgy and addictin'. He's the only other official Biz-e-Bee Publications writer so far and you have to be better than me to make the cut!

Brace yourself! His name is King Pharaoh and he's from Boston. This story is a finger that leads to an arm that leads to a phenomenal body of works this man has created. trust me! watch for him! this story is called...

THE RAPE CLUB

by

KING PHARAOH

©2017

Fellas, have you ever thought about taking the pussy? Keep it all the way real. It's just me and you right now, and I'm not going to tell anybody. Besides, it's not a crime to fantasize about it. It's only when you act upon it that things get complicated. So again, have you thought about it?

If so, what does your rape fantasy consist of? Do you get off overpowering her physically? Maybe it's the horrified look in her eyes as you barbarically rip her clothes off her. Do you like to give her a few smacks before you take it? Maybe you like it when, after all the kicking and screaming, she finally submits and gives into you fucking her brains out.

Now let's not get it twisted Ladies, this thing works both ways. Have you ever wished that your man would get on some caveman shit and just take the pussy without asking? Maybe your fantasy is to be held hostage in your house by five black guys with ten inch dicks and they're repeatedly raping you in front of your bound and gagged husband. Then again you might be one of those females that like to watch other females get raped.

If watching, reading, or hearing about rape fantasies excites you, don't feel ashamed because you aren't alone. See, we all have a dark side, some are darker than others. What makes the dark side so taboo is that there are no rules or limits. It's totally uninhibited and that's what makes it so dangerous because if you lose control of your dark side, it'll consume you. When that happens, you become capable of some sick and twisted shit but at the same time that's the lure of it. The thrill of playing so close to insanity is the ultimate aphrodisiac for some of us.

This story is for those who like to embrace their dark sexual desires.

The Phone Call

It was about 10:30 on a Friday night. I'd been in the house for a week straight, waiting on a phone call. I passed the time with my boy smoking weed, drinking Henny and breaking in the new Madden '09.

"Ayo, you got a call." My boy Romeo said as he tried to pass me the cordless phone.

"Can't you see I'm busy?!" I said, fighting with the PlayStation controller.

"Ayo Taboo, this fool has been waiting for you to call all week, but now he's too busy to speak to your fine white ass."

"Chill, let me get that!" I said frantically, reaching for the phone.

"Yeah, that's what I thought. Damn, I don't know what you did Taboo, but this fool wouldn't leave the house until you called."

Romeo held out the phone, and before I could grab it he snatched it back.

"Look at you punk, this bitch got you strung out."

"Give me the fuckin' phone!" I threw the remote controller at him and snatched the cordless out of his hands. "Ay, don't fuck my game up either."

I grabbed the Garcia out of the ashtray, stepped over the coffee table and headed to the kitchen.

"White girl lover!" Romeo shouted.

"Fuck you!" I took a couple of hits off the weed before saying. "What's up, where the fuck you been at!?"

Even though I'd been smoking weed all night, my heart was beating like crazy.

"Sorry Daddy, I had to make sure everything was set. Are you ready?"

"I've been ready for a week."

"You nervous?"

"You muthafuckin' right I'm nervous. If this shit goes wrong and this bitch goes to the police they're going to put me under the jail." I took another two hits off the Garcia. "And with a rape charge, muthafuckas will be at me everyday in there!"

"Daddy, don't worry. I won't let anything happen to you."

"Yeah right." I was pacing back and forth sweating like I'd just run a marathon.

"So do you want to forget about it?"

That was my out right there. I could've walked away right then and there and went back to my life before Taboo.

My life wasn't bad before Taboo either. I was doing it big. I was making about $2,500 a day off the crack shit and fucking a different bitch every night. It was just this bitch put me on to some wild shit and because of it I didn't want to go back to life before her.

"Nah, lets do this."

"That's my daddy." Taboo purred. "Meet me at my house."

"A'ight."

"And if everything goes right I want you to meet some friends of mine."

"Friends?"

"Yeah."

"I thought I met all your friends."

"I'm not talking about the girls I strip with. I got some other friends I want you to meet."

"Why haven't I met them before?"

"You weren't ready."

"Whatever. What time do you want me to meet you?"

"Right now and wear all black."

Freaky ass Snowbunny

Romeo gave me shit about bouncing on him for a snowbunny. But if he only knew Taboo like I did he'd bounce too. Hold up, before I go any further, I got to tell you about this bitch.

When I first met Taboo it was at the strip club. Romeo introduced me to her. Man, I didn't know what the fuck I was getting myself into. All I saw was a bitch with a body like Jessica Biel, tits like Pamela Lee and looked like Christina Aguilera in the face. I was just trying to get my fuck on but it turned into a whole lot more.

Taboo ended up being like no other girl I'd ever stuck my dick in. She did all the freaky things guys wished their girls did without me having to ask her. She liked playing with herself while she watched me fuck her friends. It was because of her that I'd fucked all the baddest strippers in West Mass.

Another thing, this bitch loved the taste of my nut so much she begged me to cum on her food before she ate it. Then she made my dream of standing over a chick and pissing on her come true. She told me I could shit on her if I wanted to. Romeo was right this bitch had me strung out. I never knew I was into all that crazy shit. You know, not many black people get down like that. All jokes a side though, this bitch brought the R-Kelly out of me.

Every time we got together she'd come up with something freakier than the last time. It wasn't just the fact that the pussy was off the chain. It was the mental fuck game that really had me open.

How it all started.

Me and Taboo had been seeing each other for a minute. I'd eventually cut off all my other bitches because they couldn't measure up. Plus when I wasn't with her I thought about her all the time, and when I was with her I didn't want her to go.

I remember the day shit got really crazy. We were at my house all day. Taboo had just finished swallowing my nut for the third time.

As she looked at me with her Caribbean blue eyes she asked, "Have you ever took some pussy?"

"What the fuck did you just say?"

"Have you ever took some pussy? You know, raped a girl?"

Without thinking I smacked the shit out of her. "Bitch, do I look like I have to take some pussy!?"

Taboo grabbed the side of her face as her eyes teared up. "I'm sorry Baby. It was just a question."

"Why would you ask me some dumb ass shit like that?"

"I was just curious."

I grabbed the clipped blunt, lit it and took two huge pulls. Taboo had me hot with her. I would've smacked her ass again but between the weed and her sucking my dick, I was too tired to do anything. Taboo wiped the tears from her eyes and came up and laid her head on my chest.

"I'm not saying you have to take pussy. I know how bitches can act sometimes. They'll tease and tease and not give it up or they'll use a guy to take them shopping acting like they were going to give it up but don't. I'm a stripper. I see it happen all the time. I've even done it a couple of times. All I'm saying is did you end up taking the pussy because of it?"

When she put it like that it made me think. I ran into several bitches playing head games like that. So if that was the case, me and Romeo roughed off plenty of pussy like that especially when we were drunk.

"So what if I took some pussy, what's the big deal?"

Taboo looked at me with this lustful look in her eyes that sent a chill straight to my dick.

"Tell me about it."

"Tell you what?"

"Tell me how you took it." Taboo rolled on her back and started massaging her pussy. "Go head, tell me."

I'd never done no shit like that before. We weren't even going to fuck and my dick was hard as shit. "You sure you want to hear this shit?"

"Yes." she moaned.

"A'ight. There was this bitch named Vanessa Rodriguez. Bad little shorty from Appleton St. She was one of those chicks that liked to smoke up all the weed and drink anything she could get her hands on and she never gave up the pussy."

"Mmmmm, go on." Taboo moaned.

"So what me and Romeo did was crush up four ecstasy pills and laced the weed and her drink with it. Ayo, the bitch got so fucked up it was crazy."

"What did y'all do to her?"

"What did we do to her? You mean what didn't we do to her. We fucked that bitch for eight hours straight."

"Ohhhh, tell me another one pleaseeeee."

I went on and told her a couple more stories about how I took some pussy and she loved every bit of it. As she played with her pussy she asked questions like, "Did you rip her clothes off? Did you smack her? Did you make her suck your dick?" And so on and so on. It seemed the rougher I was with the girls in my stories the harder Taboo came.

Taboo loved the stories so much that she had to hear one everytime we fucked. One time after I'd finish fucking her in the ass I asked her. "Ayo, Taboo tell me how in the fuck does me telling you how I took pussy turn you on?"

"I don't know why I get off on it so much. I just do. To tell you the truth I don't want to know why either."

"Why not?"

"Because it might take all the fun out of it."

My First Taste

Up until that point I was doing it all for Taboo, because I liked seeing her get off on some perverted shit. But all that changed when she asked me what I liked about taking pussy. Suddenly the spotlight was on me.

"Come on, tell me what turns you on when you take it." Taboo slid a black dildo in and out of her pussy. "Mmmm, I tell you what, I'll tell you what I like and you tell me what you like about it okay?"

"A'ight you first."

"Okay, I like hearing a girl beg with all her might. It gets my pussy so wet hearing her say. No! Stop it! Please don't hurt me! I'll do whatever you ask. Ohhhh! Yes, I love hearing them beg." Taboo started working the dildo in and out of her pussy faster and harder "Oooh! It's your turn."

I couldn't think of anything on the spot so I closed my eyes and thought about a time I roughed some pussy off. The first one that came to my mind was when I got this girl Cheryl in the VIP section of the G-Club. I was drunk as shit off Wild Irish Rose. She kept on sitting on my lap grinding her pussy into my dick. When I went to feel her up she slapped my hands away. After an hour of that shit I grabbed her by the throat. The terrified look in her eyes got my dick so hard.

Taboo saw that I was smiling.

"What are you thinking about Baby?"

Gradually I opened my eyes. "I like that terrified look in their eyes when they know I'm about to take it."

"Tell me again, but this time jerk your dick for me."

So I did. The more I spoke about it the faster I jerked my dick and the more I realized I got off on this sick perverted shit too. Me and Taboo went back and forth telling each other what we liked about taking pussy as we masturbated together.

"I like it when the guy rams his cock in the girls asshole and she screams so loud it hurts your ears."

"I like smacking them a few times before making them suck my dick."

"I like that too." Taboo moaned. "Oh God! I really fucking like that!"

I was open off of our masturbating sessions like a teenager who smoked weed for the first time. We did it every chance we got and anywhere we could. When we couldn't be with each other we'd masturbate over the phone while taking turns telling each other stories.

Just Like a Gateway Drug

We went on for about a month and some change until we both began to run out of stories. Then Taboo would make her stripper friends tell us times they were raped while we masturbated right there in front of them. Some of them would end up crying after they told us what happened, but we didn't give a fuck.

As sick as that shit may sound it wasn't enough for Taboo and if it wasn't enough for her then it wasn't enough for me. So Taboo came up with this idea to join a group called Victims of Rape. They met every Sunday night at the church in the Flats. Taboo pretended to be a rape victim and I was her understanding boyfriend, there to comfort her through her so called terrified experience. There was at least

25 other females in the group. The young counselor made every single one of them talk about their rape in detail. Me and Taboo sat there loving every bit of it. Afterwards we'd both be so horny we couldn't wait until we got home. We'd fuck ourselves into a coma right there in the church's parking lot.

Believe it or not the initial high from telling each other stories and hearing others tell their stories began to wear off. I mean we still got off on them but it wasn't like the first time. Then again nothing is as good as the first time. So like stone cold junkies we started chasing that high. The thrill of it all was nothing more than a gateway drug that took us to the next level, which was actually seeing it.

We went to every adult movie store looking for porn flicks with rape themes. We found a couple but that only wet our appetite.

Being able to see the rapes was a more intense high, way better than just hearing about them. Even though I knew they weren't real, they had all the elements of the real thing. I could see the terrified look in their eyes that got my dick so hard. Their screams and pleas as they begged their rapist to stop sounded authentic. Even the slaps to the face sent chills throughout my body. We burnt through the few DVDs we had like wild fire. Taboo went on the net and found some sweet sites called Rape.tv, SavageRape.com, and ScreamandCream.com. We had tapped into an unlimited supply of our drug of choice and if it was humanly possible we would had definitely overdosed. Have you ever heard of the saying *nothing good last forever?* Shit, in our case it only lasted about four or five months. It wasn't that we were getting bored, it was just things that didn't bother me before about it, was starting to bother me like knowing what I was watching was fake. Although I didn't say anything I knew where all this was heading. It had gotten to the point that every time I went to sleep I dreamed of taking pussy.

Then the bitch got crazy on me. This shit was starting to fuck with Taboo too. She started saying all kinds of crazy shit out of her mouth.

"You know what Baby?"

"What?"

"I'd love to see you in action. I get so damn wet at the thought of you taking some pussy for me."

Taboo was dead serious too. This bitch actually wanted me to rape a girl so she could watch. I always wondered how the fuck did we get to that point so fast. Before, I had a grip on things. The line between fantasy and reality was as clear as black and white. But all that was changing right before my eyes. Taboo was becoming more aggressive by the day. And her words blurred the line between fantasy and reality until I couldn't tell the difference between the two. One time we were in the Holyoke Mall getting something to eat. There was this fine ass Puerto Rican female at the table next to us. I could tell by her name tag she worked at the Aeropostle, but I couldn't read her name. She had a young J-Lo look with a fat ass, and some nice tits. Every once in a while I'd catch her stealing a look at me.

"You like that?"

"She a'ight."

"Would you take that pussy for me if I wanted you to?"

"You a freaked out bitch for real, yo."

209

"Don't act like I'm the only one. You know you want to do it as much as I want you to."

"You think?"

"No, I know." Taboo smiled. "Look at her, she probably will enjoy it as much as we will."

"How you figure that?"

"What girl wouldn't like your ten inch cock pounding their pussy to death?"

I smiled.

"It's simple, God wouldn't have gave her a body like that. She's built to take dick, Daddy, if she likes it or not."

Ridiculous as that may sound now, given the frame of mind this bitch had me in, it made perfect sense to me.

"Then lets do it then."

Taboo looked at me then seductively bit her bottom lip. "Really?"

"What are you scared?"

"No, I think I just came on myself." Taboo put her long hair into a ponytail. "How are we going to take it?"

"We'll follow her until she goes to the bathroom."

No sooner than I said that the Puerto Rican chick gathered her bags and headed towards the bathroom. I figure she'd have to go sooner than later because she had an empty king size cup of soda sitting in front of her. Me and Taboo looked at each other. This bitch was so excited that her nipples were poking through her bra and shirt.

Then she had that look that had my dick so hard that I had to adjust it before I stood up.

"Come on she's getting away."

We fell about twenty feet behind her and all bullshit aside, Shorty had a fat ass. I felt like a lion stalking my prey. My adrenaline was pumping, my palms were sweaty and tiny beads of sweat dotted my forehead. This shit was really happening. I was going to take some pussy right there in the mall.

The Puerto Rican female headed to the bathrooms in the Cafe Square. That was when we started closing in on her. I figured I'd grab her from behind, cover her mouth and drag her into one of the janitor's closets. I could've gotten away with it but she didn't turn into the bathroom. She kept going straight and entered into a dark hallway that goes along the back of the stores. There was nobody back there at all and ironically the darkness made me feel safe.

She peeked over her shoulder every ten or so steps.

Suddenly, she stopped and said, "Excuse me you're not supposed to be back here. It's for employees only."

I didn't say shit. I just picked up the pace. That was when she figured something wasn't right, because she turned to run. But before she could take her third step I was already on top of her.

"Get her!" Taboo growled.

"Help!! Get off of me!!!"

This bitch was kicking, scratching and screaming her ass off. I smacked the shit out of her. It dazed her for a bit but she still kept fighting, so I smacked her again and that took all the fight right out of her. Then I threw her down onto some empty boxes.

"That's it Baby. Take that pussy!!"

"Oh God please don't hurt me! Please, I have a little girl." she cried. "I'll do whatever you want. Please just don't hurt me!"

Between Taboo in my ear routing me on like a cheerleader and the Puerto Rican chick given me that fear of God look that got my dick so hard, it turned me into a monster. I started ripping her clothes off like a crazed lunatic and it drove me even crazier that she gave in.

"Fuck that bitch! Tear that pussy up!"

Within seconds I had my dick in one hand and the other pressed against the lips of her pussy. Her thick brown nipples rose and fell with each deep terrified breath she took. I thought her eyes were going to fallout of her head they were opened so wide. This bitch was mine for the taking.

"Do it damn it! Shove your cock in her cunt!"

I had this bitch spread eagle on the ground and the only thing stopping me from putting my dick in her was me. I was at the line where fantasy met reality and once I stuck my dick into her there was no going back and I think that was what had my heart beating so hard against my chest.

"I can't do it!"

"What?"

"I can't do it." I sat up.

"Why not?"

"I just can't! Fuckin' with you is going to get me locked up!"

Taboo looked like she wanted to cry as she walked away. The Puerto Rican girl thanked me a thousand times as she quickly gathered her clothes and took off in the opposite direction.

Withdrawals

Taboo stopped fucking with me after that day. She wouldn't return my calls or answer the door when I went by her spot. All her stripper friends I fucked wouldn't even speak to me. The bitch cut me all the way off and that shit had me in my feelings hard. Being the player I was, I wasn't going to sweat no bitch. There were millions of bitches out there, fuck Taboo, I didn't need her. I'd just find me another bitch and put her on to this rape shit like Taboo put me on to it.

Yeah right, most of the females I approached looked at me like I was crazy. The ones that were with it only did it because I wanted them to and not because they were into it. It didn't have the same affect.

I ended up going through it over Taboo. I didn't eat shit. I wasn't hustling or nothing. I wasn't even smoking weed anymore. The rape movies me and Taboo used to watch didn't have the same effect without her there. I was missing the hell out of that crazy ass white bitch. Especially the sick perverted sex we had.

Finally, my boy Romeo told me to go talk to her. I told him she asked me to do something crazy and I said no. He said if she had me this fucked up I should just do it. So finally I laid my pride to the side and went to the strip club Taboo danced at. Taboo saw me as soon as I walked through the door and did her best to avoid me. Every time I waved her over she'd roll her eyes and turn the other way. Later, I caught her giving a guy a lap dance. I had her cornered. There was nowhere for her to dip.

"Yo, let me holla at you when you're done."

"What do you want?" she replied with an attitude.

"Bitch, just come and find me when you're done."

Taboo let another hour pass before she came over.

"Make this fast, I'm busy."

I took a sip of my beer to clear my throat. "Up until I was about to rape that chick in the mall, we were walking a fine line between fantasy and reality."

"And?"

"I was afraid to cross that line. If I did, there was no going back to fantasyland. It would be like a heroin addict trying to get a heroin high from weed."

"I don't know what you were told, but fantasyland is for kids. I know you heard the saying *there is nothing like the real thang baby.*"

"That's easy for you to say. You're not the one crossing the line."

"Hey wait a minute, wasn't I right there with you?"

"Yeah, but I was the one going to put in all the work."

"What are you so afraid of?"

"Going to jail for rape."

"Over three quarters of rapes go unreported. Do you know why? It's because when the shit makes it to court, they make the victims look like sluts."

"Yeah, I heard that somewhere."

"Then what the fuck are you really afraid of?"

I took another sip of my beer and paused as I watched a stripper twirl from the top of the pole to the bottom. "I'm afraid I won't be able to control myself after I take my first piece of pussy. What if it turns me in to some sick ass muthafucka?"

"If you haven't figured it out by now, you're already a sick muthafucka."

"You got an answer for everything don't you?"

"No, because if I did, I'd have an answer to why you're wasting my time right now."

"I didn't come here to waste your time."

"So what's up then?"

"It's whatever with me."

"You going to bitch up on me again?"

"Just set the shit up and give me a call."

That lustful stare in her eye returned and because of it, so did the chill it sent to my dick.

Ain't Nothing Like The Real Thang

So now you know why I was waiting in the house for her call and how she had me out. It was a little after 11:00pm when I pulled up to Taboo's crib. She was already out front, dressed in an all black cat suit. She climbed in the truck, gave me a kiss on the cheek and asked, "You ready to take some pussy for me?"

"Yeah, I'm ready. Where we headed?" I tried to act as cool as possible on the surface, because underneath I was going to pieces.

"Downtown Springfield." Taboo being the good bitch she was sensed my nervousness. "Lean back a little bit." She said, so I did.

She undid my belt buckle, unzipped my pants and pulled my dick. She jerked it a little and swallowed as much as she could. The whole ride to Springfield she sucked me off not once coming up for air. Before we reached Springfield I had busted two nuts in her mouth and almost a third. "Feel better?"

"No bullshit, I needed that."

"Yeah, I thought so." she licked her lips. "Let me know if you want some more."

It was a warm summer night and the streets were packed with people. I parked in the downtown parking garage and headed out on foot. We stopped at a bar for some drinks before catching a cab up to the Mardi Gras strip club.

The Mardi Gras was packed as always. There weren't any seats by the stage so we sat by the bar.

"Is this bitch a stripper?" I asked.

"No she sells coke and x-pills to the girls."

"Why did you pick her?"

"Because she has a nice body and plus she has warrants. If the police catch her she got to do five years."

"So no matter what, she ain't going to the police."

"Bingo, so you don't have to worry about going to jail."

"Where's she at?"

"Right over there."

Taboo was right, the chick had a nice body. She was fat in all the right spots and slim in all the right spots. She had curly black hair that draped down over her shoulders and she was cute in the face.

"You sure know how to pick them."

"You like?"

"Fuck yeah, so how we going to do this?"

"Since I know her I'm going to go over and kick it with her. The bitch loves to do shots and lines of coke back to back. Plus when she gets started she can't stop. In about 30 min. to an hour I'm going to tell her the police are out front looking for her. With all that coke in her system it'll have her so paranoid the bitch might jump out of the window. But I'll be there to lead her out the back into the nice dark alley."

"And you want me to take it from there."

"Yesss." Taboo moaned in my ear. "I have only one request."

"What?"

"Fuck her in that fat ass of hers."

"I was going to do that anyway. So what do you want me to wait here or what?"

"Don't worry I'm going to have someone keep you company." Taboo gave me a kiss on the cheek and headed off. A few minutes later a light skinned black chick came over with a freshly opened bottle of Patron.

"Hi, Taboo told me to keep you company."

"She did huh?"

"Yep so why don't you come with me to the back." She grabbed my hand and led me into the private lap dance section. "Do you want me to do anything specific?"

"Yeah, put this dick in your mouth."

"I was hoping you'd ask me to suck it."

She handed me the bottle. I sat down on the sofa and she fell to her knees. "Taboo told me you had a big dick."

The bitch was a pro. Even though I knew I wasn't going to bust, it still felt good just to have my dick in her mouth. A couple more strippers came into the private section along with some guys in tow.

"What's up?" one of them said.

"What's up?" I replied after guzzling a mouth full of Patron. I didn't pay them any attention after that. My mind was on taking some pussy. I wasn't nowhere as nervous as I was in the mall, thanks to Taboo's and this bitch's head job. The Patron was doing a job on its own. It felt like I was drinking liquid ecstasy with Viagra. I had never had Patron before, but I doubt it made you feel the way I was feeling. My dick looked like it grew three inches. My blood felt like nitro pulsing through my veins. I took deep breaths to control the overwhelming feeling to put my fist through the wall.

"Ayo, you a'ight over there?" one of the dudes asked.

"I'm good. I'm real fucking good."

I grabbed the back of the bitch's head and forced it down on my dick. It made her gag to the point she teared up, but like a good little hoe she didn't resist. I would've fucked her mouth to death but some chick stuck her head in and said, "Taboo said to meet her out back."

The alley was more fucked up then I expected. The dumpsters were buried in all kinds of trash. You could hear the broken glass crunching under every foot step you took. Then there was the smell that stunk so bad it made me dizzy.

Suddenly, the back door to the club burst opened and my heart instantly went into overdrive as I ducked behind the dumpster.

"No, don't go that way stupid, go that way!" Taboo pushed my prey deeper into the alley where I was waiting like a wolf licking its fangs.

"But, but." the drunken bitch slurred as she stumbled closer and closer.

"But nothing, go before the police see you!"

That was all it took. She turned and tried to run but fell two or three times before getting to me. I let her pass me a little before I came up behind her. I grabbed her and dragged her back behind the dumpster. There was no hesitation nervousness or second thoughts about what I was going to do. Before it was about not crossing the line and not being able to go back to fantasyland. Fuck fantasyland and fuck that line!

"Ahhhhhhh!!!!!!!" she screamed with all her might but I was prepared this time with a piece of duct tape I had on the back of my wrist. I spun her around and backed handed the shit out of her. Then I grabbed her by the throat and forced her to look me in the eyes. There it was that look of fear that got my dick hard as a muthafucka. The look of helplessness in her eyes that brought out the animal in me.

She wore a tube top and a mini-skirt. So it only took a few seconds to tear it off of her. She had big tits with tiny pink nipples but that wasn't what I came for. I turned her around, bent her over pushing her face into some torn open trash bags and went straight into her asshole. She had submitted long ago because there was nothing she could do but let me do what I wanted and that is what I did.

"FLOP! FLOP! FLOP! FLOP! FLOP! FLOP! FLOP!"

I was tearing her ass up from behind. She grabbed on to the dumpster to brace herself. I didn't hold her by her hips either, I had reached under her and grabbed her tits and used them as handles.

"FLOP! FLOP! FLOP! FLOP! FLOP! FLOP! FLOP!"

"Fuck that ass Baby!" Taboo was standing off to the side with her camcorder in one hand and the other hand in her pants. "Rape that bitch!"

I punished her asshole so hard she pissed on herself and fell to the ground. I was going to pull her ass back up and give her some more but Taboo said, "Baby lets go I hear somebody coming!"

I could hear glass crunching under more than one set of footsteps. I pulled my gun out because I wasn't going to jail for rape, fuck that!

"No Baby let's go!" Taboo pulled me by my arm deeper into the alley until we popped out the other side. She had her car parked with the keys in it. We got in, hit the highway and was out.

Ain't This a Bitch

Back at Taboo's place I was so amped up that I couldn't sit still for nothing. My heart felt like a cannon going off in my chest. I felt more alive than the time I shot somebody. There was no getting around it. I was addicted.

"How did it feel?" Taboo asked as she rushed to unzip my pants. She was just as amped as I was.

"It was crazy! Hey what are you doing? You know I fucked her in the ass right?"

"I know." the nasty bitch smiled. "I'm getting rid of the evidence." She said and swallowed me whole.

After about two blunts, some Henny and Taboo sucking me off, I was more relaxed.

233

We watched the rape tape over and over. "You know what? You did real good for your first time."

"He did, didn't he?"

The sound of clapping hands made me jump up from the sofa, grab my gun and take aim into the darkness. "Who the fuck said that?"

"Hey relax killer. We aren't the police." from the darkness of the kitchen emerged four guys and two girls. All of them wore black outfits with expressionless white masks on their faces. The females wore the same cat outfit as Taboo had on and their hair was pulled back in a tight pony tail just like Taboo's.

"Seven, you said you weren't going to approach him until I said he was ready."

"I changed my mind. After that performance in the alley, I had to meet him in person."

"He isn't ready yet."

"If he isn't ready now, he'll never be."

"What the fuck are y'all talking about?!" I yelled.

The one Taboo called Seven, took a seat in the Lazy Boy directly in front of me, and since he was doing all the talking, he was the one I pointed the gun at. The two females sat down on the floor at his feet and the others sat where ever they could.

"If you put the gun down I'll tell you everything you want to know."

"It's okay, put the gun down. These were the friends I was telling you about."

Taboo put herself in between Seven and the gun. She slowly reached up and grabbed the barrel and lowered it. "Trust me, it's okay."

"Now let's talk."

"What the fuck do we have to talk about?" I barked.

"I'm here to make you an offer."

"What kind of an offer?"

"What if I said you could get paid for what you did back in the alley?"

"How do you know about that?"

"We've been keeping an eye on you. Come to think about it we have a lot of time invested in you. Honestly, after the freeze up in the mall I didn't think you'd come around after that. But Taboo said to just give you some time, voila! Here you are."

I gave Taboo the look of death, and she looked the other way.

"Don't be mad at her. She was only doing her job. Taboo is a recruiter, and she's good at it."

"Maybe a little too good." I growled as I clenched my fist.

"Yeah maybe she is, but you'll get over it, they all do, right fellas?" the other guys all nodded their heads at me."

"This bitch was playing me the whole time. Why?"

"Our business is expanding and we heard from one our members that you'd be a perfect candidate. So I sent Taboo at you. She has a way of bringing the sick twisted perverted monster out in anybody. It wasn't like she did it all by herself."

Seven snapped his fingers. One of his boys removed his hood and then took off his mask.

"You remember me?" it was the young rape counselor from the rape group me and Taboo had joined.

"That whole set up was fake?"

"Every bit of it."

One of the females removed her mask. "Remember me?" it was the Puerto Rican girl I was about to rape in the Holyoke Mall. "I had to beg Seven to let you rape me with that big fucking cock of yours and you freezed up on me. You owe me big Papi."

Another one of the guys removed his mask. When I saw his face, it fucked me up. It was my boy Romeo. "I'm the one that told them about you."

Seven and the rest removed their masks. I recognized all of them from one place or another. Seven was the one that said what's up to me at the strip club. The last girl removed her mask and it was the girl I had just raped. "You better had remember me." She said.

"So for real I never raped nobody?"

"Fuck no! Are you crazy, that's against the law. You can go to jail for that shit. What kind of sick muthafuckas do you think we are?" they all laughed.

I didn't think it was funny. I was still hot. "So what the fuck you want from me?"

The laughter stopped. Seven saw that I was still upset.

"We want you to join our club."

"And what does this club do?"

"We get paid to make rape fantasies for men, women, gays and anybody that wants it to come true. There's a lot of people out there that like to play on the dark side of sexual desire and they pay good money for it too."

"Are you serious?"

"Dead serious. This is a business. We have lawyers, contracts to be signed, mandatory AIDS testing and a shit load of other things we have to do. Believe it or not we are incorporated too."

"How does it work?"

"We're contacted through various channels and sometimes we contact potential customers. We never meet them directly. We got other people for that. They give the scenario they want and we make it happen. It cost $25,000 up front and $2,500 each additional rapist, plus tax. Uncle Sam got to get his cut."

"$25,000 up front?"

"Beats selling crack." Romeo cut in.

"Now there's a catch. This is the only time we're going to make this offer for you to join. If you don't you'll never hear from us again. That includes Romeo and Taboo. So what's it's going to be?"

Everybody looked at me especially Taboo. I was still heated at that bitch. Then there was my boy Romeo, who knew the whole time and didn't say shit.

Seven rose and so did the others. He put on his mask and so did the others including Taboo.

"Once we walk out that door it's a wrap."

One by one they walked out the door. Taboo came up to me and tried to give me a hug but I stepped back. She dropped her head and said, "I never wanted it to end like this."

"Bitch get the fuck outta my face."

Taboo walked to the door, turned around and blew me a kiss, said, "Bye, bye." and closed the door.

I started pacing back and forth. A part of me believed I made the right decision. The other part of me believed that if I didn't catch them I would regret it. Then I thought. Fuck it, it was too late to turn back now. I ran to the door to catch them. Soon as I opened the door they were all standing there looking at me.

"You called it again Taboo." Seven said as he pulled out another white mask, and tossed it at me.

"Welcome to the Rape Club."

I hit the road for a couple of days headin' west. Whenever I felt tired I would just pull over to a rest stop and take a nap for a few hours then hit the highway again. I came around the top way of the country. I passed by Walla Walla prison in Washington state. I passed right through rainy Seattle and went south into Portland. By that time I couldn't drive any further without a good night's sleep so I stopped at what looked like a cool little clean hole in the wall motel. When I got out of the car I heard music comin' from a bar on the other end of the parkin' lot. Before I paid for the room I figured I'd go over and run some alcohol through my system to relax me. When I walked in I noticed that it was kind of a all-white locals-only type of place with the country western singer Carrie Underwood's music playing over the speakers.

There was a mechanical bull buckin' the hell out of this one white girl. I looked up just as she was bein' flung into the air and onto her ass. She got up and shook it off like it was nothin'. She had on brown cowboy boots, a tan dress with white lace around the trim, a red shirt and a red bow in her hair. I knew I was in the wrong spot and was about to about-face when I saw a brotha come out of the bathroom. Then I saw a white girl come out behind him. She came out of the men's room. I didn't have to think hard about what my boy had just been into. I thought to myself, shit, this may be the perfect place for a freak like myself. I went to the bar and ordered a drink. I threw the whole thing back in one long gulp. When I looked up the brotha was takin' a seat next to me. I told him that I was just passin' through town and there were two things that I wanted to know if he could possibly help me out with. One was, if there was possibly an underground of erotic writers I could tap into and secondly, if I could tap into some of this Caucasian ass spread so lavishly around the place. I had a quick vision of beatin' some white ass cheeks into a hot pink color. And if her pussy was wet and wouldn't quit then maybe to a purple pulp.

I snapped back into the present, he was saying somethin'. I missed it.

"Huh?" I said.

"I said you're in the right city. They don't call it Porkland for nothing. Per capita, we have more strip clubsbs here than any other metropolitan city in the country. That's if you wanna pay for it but I know a few white girls right here that need it beat up. My girl," he said, noddddin' over to the white girl he had came out of the bathroom with. "won't allow me to fuck none of them and everybody around here knows everybody around here. But my girl is my rock, she gives me everything I need, lets me put it anywhere I want, so I don't really need to mess around but I encourage you to get your fill Bill."

"Biz, my name is Biz."

"Yeah whatever. You want me to hook you up?"

"Do I need to answer that?"

"I'ma tell you like this, the girls in here have already been checking you out, believe me. Just have a couple of drinks and by the end of the night you'll have a couple of options, trust me. Oh, where are you staying?"

"We'll, I was goin' to get a room across at the lil motel over there."

"Well you may not have to do that. It depends on what you want to do but a lot of these women live alone and most of them live in a small town on the coast, well there's actually three small towns together which are about two hours from here. There's only a thousand people between the three towns but you'd be surprised at the things that go down out there."

"Sounds interestin'"

"It is, but it can be borin' at times too. Actually, it's borin' most of the time. That's how we like to live."

He went back over to his girl and downed a shot of liquor that sat on the table. So anyway, I kicked it by the bar and ordered a drink.

Before the drink was made, this white chick sat next to me and slid me a piece of paper with her number on it. She was kind of busted in the face. I didn't want no parts of her. I shined her on with some nonchalant responses. After a while she got the picture and went back to her friends by the pool table.

About twenty minutes later a hot brunette white chick with nice tits comes straight over to me and says, "I live in a little piece of paradise near the coast and if you come home with me I promise to give you something you'll never forget."

She said it with the cutest, devilish grin on her face. I didn't need to hear much more. I followed her outside. She finished downin' a small bottle of beer and threw the bottle on the roof of the place. I went to get my car and when I pulled up I saw her and another pretty girl gettin' into a white Mustang. JACKPOT JACKPOT JACKPOT! I thought. I followed these girls for two hours flirtin' on the road most of the way. There were a lot of curves and crazy twists in the road. Most of the time I just stayed behind them because I could tell they knew the terrain well. It was pretty dark for the most part but I could still see the magnificence of the landscape. It was a get away of get aways. I could tell that it was fall season by the colors of the trees, a wider array of colors of fall leaves than I ever saw before, especially, ever in L.A. My mind began to travel twice as fast as my miles per hour on some wild fantasies about fuckin' these two girls. I could imagine one takin' care of my left side and one takin' care of my right. One caterin' to my front, massagin' my pecs and absbs and one rubbbbin' my back down. Oh yeah, what fun we are goin' to have. Finally, we came out into a clearin' and a view opened up to the ocean. Damn, I liked it, not many places can I see this facet of life. We hit a couple of corners and pulled up to a buildin' with a store on one side and an apartment on the other. "Finally, we're here." I said to myself. I was gettin' ready to park when I noticed the girl in the passenger seat get out and run around the side of the buildin'. Then I noticed the wheels of the Mustang begin to roll. The car stopped and the window came down. She stuck her hand out of the window then signaled for me to follow her. Shit! My fantasy disintegrated before my eyes. Well, she still promised me somethin' I would never forget. I thought. I followed her around a few bends and we pulled into a yard in front of a house. You could barely see the house for all the trees in front. When we walked into the house there was a man standin' in the livin' room. I immediately thought about black dude at the bar tellin' me that a lot of shit goes down around here. Oh shit! This broad is on some other shit! I thought about how far I just drove. Damn!

She introduced us, we exchanged greetings. He was cool. He offered me a drink. A red flag went up in my head. I kept my guard up. I was too far out the way and too tired to get back. I chilled out on the couch and took a big swig of the beer. She went into the room and came back with a laptop. She sat next to me and began to read a story about some dude named Troy that she fell in love with and had the best sex of her life. To keep it real, the way she wrote the story pulled me in. She was a damn good writer. I had found a diamond in the rough. It turns out that she wasn't fuckin' the dude and had no intention on fuckin' me either. She honestly never said she would, she was playin' with words as writers do. She had been celibate for a year or so until Troy, then when he left she

had decided to go right back into celibacy. They just had
one of those chemical reactions of souls I guess. The story
is called Nature's Secret and her name is Stormy.

Nature's Secret

by
STORMY
©2017

I let my mind wander as I hugged the curves of the mountain doing sixty miles an hour with no destination in mind. I was comfortable behind the wheel and as always, a little breathless from the magnificence of the coastline. High clouds pillowed the sky, casting shafts of filtered sunlight to the sea below.

"Rays of hope." I said aloud. Mmmmm… I wish Troy was here to see this. I've been missing him so badly. There's just something about a winter sky that brings out the melancholy in me, and the vixen. I could get into some nature loving right about now.

My clitoris tingled just thinking about the silhouette we would make with Troy's tall and hard body pressed up against mine, his gorgeous black cock straining against the worn denim of his jeans as he backed me up against an old fir tree.

Of all of my fantasies, sex outdoors was among my favorites. Just being naked in the elements stirred me emotionally. The tease of a breeze dancing across my skin, the crystal surprise of river waters between my thighs and mud oozing between my toes, all these thoughts excited me. I moaned with longing and felt my pussy growing wet between my thighs.

Oh God, what has that man done to me? I thought, chuckling at how easily aroused I was. Just the thought of his hands all over my body makes my honey flow.

Where's that tongue when I need it?

Troy and I had met only a few months ago but I was in deep and long past the point of no return. Our relationship was set up through mutual friends, Anna and Michael and I got the feeling that this affair was orchestrated strictly as a form of entertainment for the two of them. Troy was a childhood friend of Michael's who was visiting from out of town and Michael wanted to ensure his buddy got the VIP treatment while he was here. Anna is my best friend and she just wanted me to get laid properly, no strings attached, which by her definition could only be achieved by a black man and his black dick.

Ha! That man should've come wearing a skull and crossbones! I thought.

He was some kind of poison for a woman who prided herself on holding her own. Once that man got inside me, my hard won liberation scattered to the wind. All I wanted was more.

As a self-proclaimed serial monogamist, I had initially rejected the set up. Over the years I had learned that it was easier to remain celibate rather than to tangle myself up in sex without love. I needed to feel a connection to someone before I gave that part of myself away. Truthfully, I had slept with black men in the past but it had been random. They weren't players in the fantasy I was actively pursuing. Besides, the whole arrangement made me feel like I was being pimped. I had agreed to come over for dinner the following evening but I made it perfectly clear that sleeping with Troy wasn't part of the deal.

Funny how quickly I changed my mind about that! I thought, remembering our first encounter. Our alchemy was undeniable. The first time we were in the same room together the air crackled with possibility. The commingling of our opposing energies generated a current of electricity that ran from the top of my head straight to the soles of my feet. Not only was Troy physically beautiful, he was articulate, funny, and sexy as hell.

After spending several hours engaging in intelligent and provocative conversation, I found my resolve weakening. Toss in several vodka and tonics with lime, some Oregon kind bud and Troy's penetrating gaze and the rest was history.

We spent the next three days and nights coupled, communicating primarily in sighs and moans and urgent whispers. I lay stretched out beneath him, an unexplored territory begging for discovery while Troy read my body like a map, tracing its curves and peaks with his fingers, measuring distances with his tongue. His body was exquisite, perfectly cut, with defined pecs, ripped abs and strong, powerful hands. And his cock, oh Lord, never before had I seen such an impressive specimen. It was silky and smooth and stretched nine inches from his hairless balls to the magenta head he filled me with. It felt like my uterus was being displaced in order to accommodate him.

As I daydreamed, I shifted into fifth gear and leaned my head back on the headrest. Half closing my eyes I accelerated into a straightaway and thought about the first time I took him in my mouth.

We were sleeping naked in my bed on our last day together, morning sunlight spilled across the crisp white cotton sheets. Halfway between dreaming and waking I opened my eyes and turned to face him, watching the gentle rise and fall of his chest, the flutter of lashes against his cheeks. My god, he is beautiful… I remember thinking to myself. I knew a "good bye" wasn't gonna come easy. Raising myself up on one elbow, I pulled the comforter down, slowly unveiling the rest of his chiseled torso. Down his chest, tattooed in scars and indigo, past his hipbones, to the place where his cock lay nestled, sleepy and soft.

Gently throwing one leg over his, I blazed a trail of feathery kisses across his skin until I reached his penis. Lifting it with my tongue, I took him between my lips and sucked tenderly, waiting for him to respond. Within seconds, he began to swell and elongate in my mouth.

I moaned and rubbed my pussy lips against his muscular thigh as I moved slowly up and down his shaft, taking in as much as I could with deep, long pulls. I licked circles outside, around the base then moved back up to the head, tickling and teasing it with my tongue.

Troy worked his hands through my wavy, chestnut hair as he groaned with pleasure. "Yeah Baby, like that. Oh, I like it when you do it soft like that."

I was riding his thigh now, lips spread, clit engorged, sliding up and down with the rhythm of my sucking.

"Baby, I'm so close to cumming." I whispered. "Oh, god, I want you to cum with me. Cum in my mouth. Give me everything you've got."

Troy grabbed a fistful of my hair and pushed my head down, deep on his throbbing cock. Faster and faster I worked it, grinding and sucking until I felt myself about to explode.

"Okay…okay…I'm gonna cum, Babe, oh! Oh, my god!"

I felt Troy's legs stiffen, felt his cock twitch in my mouth and knew he was right there with me. With a groan, he gave one last thrust and erupted into my mouth, shooting a thick stream of hot semen down my throat. I drank it down, eagerly sucking out every last drop.

With a grin I licked my lips and said, "Mmmm… The breakfast of champions! Just wanted to give you a little something to remember me by…"

Troy stroked my head and pulled me close. "Don't you worry Baby." he said, "I won't forget you. You're my favorite white girl."

The blare of a horn from an oncoming pickup truck startled me out of my reverie and

I swerved back into my own lane. "Well, all things must pass." I said aloud, quoting one of my favorite George Harrison songs. I down shifted into fourth gear and began singing,

"Sunrise doesn't last all morning, a cloudburst doesn't last all dayseems my love is up and has left you with no warning

Its not always going to be this grey

All things must pass

All things must pass away

All things must pass

None of life's strings can last

So I must be on my way

And face another day"

Troy returned home to his life while I suffered the sweet aftershocks of his impact on mine. The relationship continued, consisting mainly of stolen moments, borrowed time and lots of cyber sex. This was a bone of contention between us, my self-imposed monogamy and his insatiable sexual urges. It pissed me off that there wasn't another man within a hundred mile radius who would ever satisfy my passions the way Troy did. In the meanwhile, I knew he hit the pussy hard in his hometown and had no intention of stopping to tend to my needs. We had argued about it this morning, long distance, and by the end of the conversation I had convinced myself I was finished. A long drive up the coast would give me the solitude I needed to clear my head and Troy wouldn't be able to reach me because I had no cellphone. Troy wanted to be able reach me anytime anywhere, but I had restrictions and my calls were accepted only at his convenience.

I signaled and got off exit 38 headed for the state park. I made my way slowly up the serpentine gravel road until I reached the trail head. Great! I thought. Not too many people. I parked the car and got out, inhaling deeply the moist earthy smells of the forest. I walked quietly along the path, carpeted with pine needles and the hush of moss and said a prayer of gratitude. Living here is to live with grace. It reminds me of how insignificant I am, how precious and small I am in comparison to the forces of nature. Troy has the same effect on me. He too, is a force of nature. My clit throbbed in agreement. I scanned the woods until I found the perfect tree, one too large to wrap my arms around.

"Okay Baby, this one's for you."

I closed my eyes and leaned up against the trunk of the tree and let my fantasies resume.

Troy slowly ran his hands up the length of my body, over my clothes, skimming over the damp mound of my plump, fat pussy up to my nipples. He pinched and tweaked the stiff little peaks until I groaned. "Ooh yeah Baby harder. Pinch me harder. Bite me until I whimper. I felt his cock swelling with each little cry of pleasure. "You like it hard, don't ya Baby?" whispered Troy, slowly grinding against me. "Well, I'm gonna fuck you so good and hard you'll be mine for life. This pussy is going to belong to me. Take off your shirt and your bra and let me look at you". I did as I was told and raised my arms seductively over my head, giving my D cup breasts a little extra lift. "Pretty sexy white girl!" said Troy, stepping back to appreciate the view. "Now take off your jeans and spread your legs. I'm gonna suck and nibble your clit until you cum and then I'm gonna bury my cock in you from behind and pound that pussy something fierce." I felt my legs grow weak with the thought of his tongue on my clit and slowly unzipped my pants, giving my hips a little wriggle as I worked them down over my long, well shaped legs. I lifted one foot first, then the other and stood naked before him. "Mmmm hmmm. Pretty as a picture." said Troy, moving in on me. Taking my face in his hands, he kissed me, his lips like ripe blueberries, all full and sweet and juicy. I felt my own juices flowing as his tongue snaked in and out of my mouth, gently at first then probing incessantly. Pressing my pelvis against him I groaned and whispered, "Ooh Baby... I want you so much... my cunt is on fire. Please, please, let me have you." Troy pulled back, smiling and said, "Don't you worry Honey. You're getting it. But first I want a taste of you." He got on his knees and spread my lips with his long tapered fingers, breathing in my delicate musk. "Oh yeah Baby. Ooh, you smell so good... sweet wet pussy just for me... c'mere and give me some of that goodness." I thrust my hips forward and let him work his black magic. He licked me slowly like an ice cream cone in long, smooth strokes. I flowered beneath his mouth, my lips opening like petals. Sinking his middle finger deep inside my fleshy walls he found my G spot and applied gentle pressure all the while flicking and teasing my swollen nubbin with the tip of his tongue. I rotated and ground my hips against his face, my hands twisting in his hair, pulling him closer. Troy increased his tempo, flicking faster and faster, keeping time with my sighs and moans until I came, my clit quivering and fluttering with sweet release. "Oh Troy... oh Babe, thank you thank you thank you." "You wanna thank me?" asked Troy. "I'll let you thank me. Turn around and pop that ass of yours up. I'ma fuck that fat pussy long and hard. We might be fucking on this tree until the seasons change. Get movin' girl!" I spread my legs a bit and bent over, wrapping my arms around the trunk of the tree, nipples scraping against the bark. I loved the feel of him coming at me from behind, his breath hot in my ear, his hands on my neck, the weight of him driving into me. "Oh, oh, oh, Troy... oh God! You're so deep inside! Oh, oh, easy! Oooh, go easy, Baby. Slow it down." Troy slowed his strokes, his cock gliding in and out of me, glistening with my juices. "Damn, girl." Thrust, withdraw, thrust, withdraw. "You so wet!" he said. Slam, withdraaaaaw. "Tell me it's mines Baby. Tell me how you ain't never been fucked so good before." He put in just the tip. "Tell me that soft, squishy pussy is mines." He inched it in a little more, then out. Troy grabbed my hair and pulled. I moaned and said, "Please oh please fuck me!" Pound! Pound! Pound! Like a Jackhammer. "Is it mine, is it mine?" he said, ramming me until his balls were slapping against my ass. "Oh God! Yes! Yes oh fuck! It's yours! I'm yours!" Troy exploded inside me at the sound of those words. He owned my pussy. I belonged to him, and he belonged to no one.

The sharp crack of breaking branches jolted me from my masturbatory pleasures and I quickly withdrew my fingers from between my creamy lips and grabbed for my jeans. Oh shit! I hope to God no one saw that erotic display. I'd hate to think I spoiled some family's Sunday-after-church outing. I laughed. Well, making love with Troy is my favorite form of worship! Damn! How could I argue with someone who makes me feel so fucking alive? He feeds my spirit, inspires me and makes me want to be a better woman. I am not about to give him up. I need to get my ass home so I can call him and apologize.

I finished dressing and began the short hike back to my car. I shivered in the fading evening sunlight, wishing I had worn a few more layers. When I reached the parking area my car was the only one left. It was kinda creepy being so deep in the forest with no one else around. Even the trees seemed lonely. As I approached my car I noticed that the left rear tire was flat. "Fuck! Fuck! Fuck! I don't have a spare and I'm gonna trash my rim riding down this crater ridden road! Damn it!" Makes me wish I had that stupid cell phone now. Well, I had no choice. I wasn't staying there. I hit the unlock button on my remote and reached for the door handle.

"Looks like you've got a little problem doncha Pretty Lady?" said a husky voice from behind me.

I whirled around, my heart beating wildly against my chest.

"Oh you scared the hell out of me! Where did you come from?"

"I've been here for awhile and haven't seen another soul. It's been kinda nice actually. Yeah, I have a little problem, maybe you can help me."

I smiled shyly at the buff, boyish-looking young man standing in front of me. He's cute. I thought. Looked like a surfer. "Nice video camera." I said. "Shooting some footage?"

Ayway, he seemed harmless enough. "Where are you parked?" I asked. "or even better, do you have a cell phone I could use?"

He smiled, slowly, teasingly. "I think we can work something out. I'll help you with your problem if you'll help me with mine. See, I saw you back there. I watched it all from beginning to end and I gotta tell ya, you were hot, lady. Mmm... mmm... those tits... those thighs... I especially loved the way you backed your ass up against that tree and arched your back. I couldn't resist stealing a few photographs.

"What the fuck!" I interrupted. Oh my God! How embarrassing! "Jesus, what are you, some kind of voyeur? A peeper? Delete those pictures now, you asshole! I'm not helping you with anything!"

He laughed menacingly. "Oh you'll help me. I know you'll help me. You'll help me 'cause you need to get that sweet ass back home to whatever man you were creaming for back there. You'll help me 'cause you wanna get out of here still breathing."

My eyes widened as I watched the man pull a long silver blade from under his sweatshirt. In one fluid motion he was on me, slamming me up against the side of the car and twisting one arm behind my back. He held the knife to my throat growling, "Just relax. Do as I say and you'll be just fine. You'll be milking every inch of sympathy you can get out of your boyfriend's cock tonight, I promise. But first, ya gotta share that sexy snatch with me. We're going to take a little walk now. And don't try to run. I promise you I'm faster."

I whimpered, "Please. I'll do whatever you say, just please don't hurt me."

I could feel his cock stiffening against my ass as he pushed me harder against the door. "I'm not gonna hurt ya Baby. I'm just looking for a little entertainment. Now, gimme the car keys and move!"

Head down, rigid with fear, I allowed the man to commandeer me back into the woods. I struggled to remember everything I'd been taught about self-defense and came up blank. All I could think about was Troy and how our last words to each other were those of frustration and disappointment. I'm getting through this. I am. Troy is the best thing that's happened to me in years. I thought. My mind was racing. I deserve another chance to tell him just how much he moves me. Please help me to be strong. I prayed silently as we walked for twenty minutes or more off the designated trail. I could hear the ocean getting louder and through the trees I caught a glimpse of the first rays of sunset. Will I ever see something so beautiful again? I wondered.

"Okay," said the man. "we're here." I lifted my head and looked around and couldn't help but gasp at the beauty. We were in an alder grove, stark, white and austere, an extreme contrast to the rest of the rainforest. It was so magical for a split second I forgot to be scared.

"Remember this place. Remember this place.

Remember this place. Come back and make it your own." I murmured to myself.

"I'm gonna let go of your arm now sweetheart and you aren't gonna move until I tell you to, isn't that right?" said the man.

He gave me a little shove as he released his grip on my arm. I stumbled to my knees and looked up imploringly. "Please you don't have to do this! I have money, you can take my car."

"I don't want any of that shit! I told you. I want what he's got. I want you to cream and moan and cum for me like you do for him. Now, get up and take off your clothes."

I stood up slowly on trembling legs and pulled my t-shirt over my head. Reaching behind my back, I unhooked my bra and set my breasts free. My nipples stiffened in the cool mist of the dusk.

"Oh yeah, what a pair of tits, big, brown areolas, rock hard nips, just begging to be bitten."

The man moved toward me with outstretched hands and cupped my breasts, bowing his head and taking a nipple between his teeth. He tugged gently at first, then bit down so hard I yelped. The man raised his head and met my eyes.

"I'm sorry. I told you, I'm not gonna hurt you. I just wanted to sample the merchandise. Now back up Darlin'. I want you just the way you were before. Legs spread and pussy dripping up against that tree. You're gonna perform, I'm gonna watch and we're both going to get off. And I'm videotaping it for my future viewing pleasure."

I could feel his dick swelling in his fatigues as he pressed me against the papery skin of the alder.

Holding the camera with one hand and his cock with the other, he then ordered me to take off my pants. Reluctantly, I unzipped and stepped out of my jeans. "Sexy bitch!" he said.

"Doesn't wear any panties! Mmmm hmmm. I like! Show me, now! Show me how you take care of yourself when your man isn't around. I wanna see that pussy glisten." I swallowed hard and took a deep breath. Okay. I thought. Relax. You can do this. Just think about Troy. Think about that long, purple headed black cock teasing your lips. I felt my clit jump in response to my imagery. Oooh, guess it really doesn't take much to turn me on. I thought. I'm gonna give this asshole a show he'll never forget.

I stared deeply into the young man's eyes and slowly ran my hands over my breasts, imagining Troy's strong hands pinching and plucking my nipples. I felt my cunt tingle with pleasure. "Ooh." I moaned, moving my hips in a slow, swaying rhythm. "Mmmm… my pussy really got wet." I snaked an arm down my belly and across my full hips, fingers barely grazing my hot, soft folds. Slipping my hands between my thighs I parted my legs, exposing the sweet, pink flesh.

"Like what you see?" I asked coyly.

The man grunted in reply, his dick throbbing in his hand. "Oh man. You are one sexy bitch! Finger fuck that pussy for me girl." He began stroking his dick with long, slow pulls. I dipped first one, then two fingers into my creamy pussy, never taking my eyes off him. I moaned and arched my back, fingers working in and out, sticky with my honey. With my other hand I greedily sought my swollen clit, teasing it out from under its hood and flicking it lightly with my fingers. "Oooh, ooh... mmm... oh, feels sooo good..." I moaned. I watched as the man increased his strokes, heard the quickening of his breath.

This guy is already close to shooting his load, I thought. 10 minutes and it's over. Thank goddess for small favors! I raced toward my climax, fingers drumming wildly on my hot button. "Ooh, oh, god…oh my god, I'm gonna cum… oh, I'm cumming, I'm cumming… ohhhhh! I bucked against my hand and watched as he closed his eyes and let go, pumping his dick furiously. "Oh Christ, oh, man, oh, you sexy sexy bitch!" he groaned. "I'm gonna explode! Aw, fuck, here I go! Uhh…uhh..uhhh…" Two or three milky spurts and it was over.

I waited while the man stood up, stuffed his dick into his pants and tossed me my car keys. "See? True to my word. You're free to leave. I'll call you a rescue."

Taking a cell phone from his pocket he called Triple A and gave my location. He cupped his hand over the receiver and said to me, "It's crazy. Usually I can't get reception when I'm in the woods but its working fine here, must be something about these trees. "Half an hour. By the time you get to the parking lot help will have arrived and I'll be long gone. Thanks for the memories. Until we meet again." and with a wave of his hand, he slipped into the shadows of the forest and disappeared.

Six grueling hours later I was standing under a scalding hot shower attempting to scrub away the humiliation of my day. I still had no idea what I was going to tell Troy, or how he would react. Maybe it's best if I play it all down, I thought. leave it up to local law enforcement. No sense in getting him all worked up when he's a thousand miles away.

I turned off the water and stepped out into a swirl of steam. I grabbed a towel, wiped off the mirror and stared at my naked reflection. Will he feel differently about me once he learns that another man's eyes and hands and mouth were on me? Will he still want me? My body flushed with shame.

"That's bullshit and you know it! Of course he will." I said aloud. "That's just your embarrassment talking." God, I hope so. I thought as I slipped into one of Troy's t-shirts, went to the kitchen and opened a bottle of pinot noir. No time to let this one breathe, I thought as I poured three inches into my glass. I gulped it down and felt the slow, peppery burn spread through my body. Ohhhh... I really needed that. I poured another glass, grabbed the bottle and retreated to my bedroom to call him.

Troy picked up on the third ring with a gruff, "Girl! Where the fuck have you been? It's midnight! You tripped on me this morning, talked all that shit about how I'm not available, then you go and be unavailable! And now you wanna call me fifteen hours later? You got me fucked up! You know I don't play that shit!"

"I know baby, I know." I interrupted, my voice cracking with emotion. "I'm sorry it's so late but God, I needed to hear your voice. Forget what I said this morning. I love you and I'm sorry I was such an ass."

I started to cry. Whether it was the wine or the sound of Troy's voice, I couldn't be sure but either way, my walls went down.

Troy sighed, indulged me for about twenty seconds then said with a hint of annoyance, "Aight, aight stop crying Stormy.

You still haven't answered me. Where the hell you been all night?"

"Troy listen," I sniffed. "that's what I've been trying to tell you. Something's happened and I need you here to take care of it. You know the cops around here aren't going to do shit. They play detective, drag their asses for a while, then hope everyone's problems go away on their own."

"Stop talking." said Troy, with quiet authority. "I don't know what the fuck happened but I can tell it's serious. I gotchu. Gimme' some time to get it together. I'll get there as soon as I can. You just get some sleep and hit me up in the morning, aight?"

"Alright."

We said our goodbyes and I hung up the phone with a smile on my face. He said he got me. I went to sleep thinking about what I would tell Troy. For now this would be me and...

NATURE'S SECRET

I couldn't resist! I had to give you another one and what better name to give the last erotic story in a book of short stories than to call it,
Gettin' Fucked In The End.

IT'S YUH BOY!!!!

Gettin' Fucked In The End

By Biz Nolastname

2017

A car stops about five cars behind Dayna's. It had been following her since she left her job as a nurse at Kaiser hospital. The car that had been following her was a silver new model Chevy Impala. It was six o'clock in the evening and the sky was turning orange as the sun lowered on the world's west side.

Dayna is 5'5", 120lbs. Her black hair hung long and straight with blonde streaks that gave her an intriguing look. She had legs that went on forever. Her butt was nice and fat with curvaceous hips to match.

Dayna parked her car and went into Trader Joe's grocery store, on the corner of 3rd Street and La Brea. She had decided to do a little shopping although she was tired from dealing with patients all day. She figured she'd go home and make dinner for one since her fiancé Robert was going to be out of town for a few more days. Robert has made a career out of bodybuilding and was in the mid-west competing. His godly body is what attracted Dayna to him. Goose bumps raised on her skin as she thought about it. She shook off the thoughts and picked up a basket then filled it with lettuce, tomatoes, avocados and a bottle of white Zinfandel wine. She went to check out.

"Good evening." says the cashier named Joyce.

"Good evening Joyce. How are you?" says Dayna.

"I can't complain. Where's your handsome man, is he not with you today?"

"No, he's out of town again."

"Will he be gone long?"

"Well, he's already been gone a couple days. I guess maybe a couple more. I miss him so much."

"Your total is $21.58. Will that be cash or charge?"

"Cash."

"Try not to miss him so much. A few days isn't that long."

"I'll try. You have a good night." Dayna said, headed towards the exit.

Once outside, she spotted her car, a midnight blue 745 LI BMW with grey interior. It sat on 22 inch wheels that were the same color of the car. She sat down in the comfortable contours of her driver's seat and placed the shopping bag on the passenger seat. There was a picture on the dashboard. It was a picture of her getting out of the pool in the Bahamas while Robert and her were on vacation. It had been a year but it was still so vivid in her mind that it felt like yesterday.

She remembered sucking his dick in the Jacuzzi late that night. Robert had sat on the edge with his feet hanging into the water. Dayna stood between his legs as she bobbed up and down on him. He was flaccid from the effect of the hot tub but she made him grow with the warmth of her mouth. She had on a two piece black and orange bikini. Dayna loved giving head. She placed her left hand flat on Robert's six-pack and stroked his dick with the other as she sucked him. Robert laid back on his elbows as she sucked and sucked and sucked. They could hear the faint but clear sound of Caribbean music in the distance. She deep throated him several times then backed off and just sucked on the tip. That made him twitch and squirm. He felt his load building up.

He whispered to her, "Vicky, if you take all my dick back in, I'll give you all my cum." She readily responded by lowering her head all the way down on him. After about ten deep strokes, he shot a thick load deep down her throat.

Dayna was now staring into the picture and salivating at the mouth from the reminiscence. She longed for Robert's touch. She put the car in drive and pulled out of her parking spot. As she drove off, she swore she could feel eyes upon her.

The man behind the wheel of the Impala quickly ducked down as Dayna made a

U-turn towards the parking lot exit. His heart was beating hard. His death grip on the steering wheel had produced fine nail marks and the palms of his hands were red as a pomegranate from the pressure. He waited a few moments then pulled out behind her. His birth name was Carlton.

Carlton had gone to college at USC with Dayna and was so infatuated with her that he kept track of her every move. Nearing the last months of school, Carlton had asked Dayna out on a date and she obliged with moderate interest. The date had gone well. Carlton had gotten paid from his job and had opted to spend the better half of it on Dayna that night. When the date had come to an end and they were headed home, Carlton suggested that they get a room anywhere of her liking but she declined him. He suggested an alternate location, like his place or even hers, yet again he was denied. That boiled his blood. He couldn't believe what a dick tease she was. The whole year at school she had smiled at him and even spoke to him on several occasions. Now after he had spent his hard earned money her true colors had surfaced. Carlton felt that she had owed him for misleading him all of this time. He had restrained himself but she almost got a beatdown and a good fucking anyway that night, instead, he took her home without saying another word. She had barely gotten out of the car when he burned rubber down her street. Carlton fumed with indignation and swore to make her pay for treating him like a trick.

Recently, he had gone to the hospital to receive a diagnosis for the chronic headaches he'd been having. On his way in, he'd noticed

Dayna coming out. He decided that to relieve the pain she had caused him had just hit number one on his priority list. It had been five years but Dayna still looked the same. She didn't even look in his direction. That pissed him off even more.

She still thinks she's all that!

Now he was hot on her trail. He could see her just up ahead at the traffic light a few cars ahead. He had fantasized about this for a while now and just the thought of it brought him to a quick arousal. He could feel himself rising fast. Visions flashed through his mind. He was standing over her. She was scared and crying. He smacked her with the back of his hand, her head swung and an earring flew into the wall and fell to the ground. She lay flat on her back helpless. He grabbed her by her blouse and ripped it open tearing the buttons.

He snatched her bra off, carelessly scratching her skin with his un-manicured nails. As the images plagued him he moved in his seat, stuck his hand in his pants and repositioned his now hard dick to relieve himself of the pressure.

"Fuckin' Bitch!" he yelled to himself out loud and continued to travel not far behind. It was 7:38pm and the sun had started to go down. Carlton figured it would get better as darkness fell and the world started to wind down. He couldn't wait, he could almost feel her.

He was parked up the street where she couldn't see him but he could see the garage door slowly close behind her car. He knows that she is in for the night. He turns off the car and waits until she's settled in before he makes a move.

In the house Dayna puts her grocery bag on the counter then goes into the living room, removes her shoes and turns on the radio. She heard the smooth tunes of 94.7 the Wave. She lights some candles and goes into the kitchen. She opens a bottle of wine and pours herself a glass. She puts it to her nose and inhales.

So sweet.

She sips it then drinks half of it down. She puts the glass down to begin preparing for her dinner. She fixes herself a filling meal complete with soup and salad on the side. Once she was done she cleans up after herself and goes into the bedroom to undress. When she is down to bra and panties she picks up the cordless phone and goes into the bathroom to run her bath water. Her thing is to add bubbles and baby oil and she likes it nice and hot.

When the water is done she gets in and releases the stress of her day.

She enjoys the quietness of her home, just soft mellow music playing in the background. Soft, hot suds caress every inch of her body. She picks up the phone and calls Robert.

He answers on the second ring. "What's up Baby?"

Dayna smiled. "Nothing, just finished eating and now I'm in the tub. I miss you and I'm not the only one. I think the girl at the market on 3rd, Joyce, you know the one that is always friendly with us, I think she has the hotts for you."

They laughed.

"We'll have to see if she wants to join us one of these days."

"Don't get hurt Stupid!"

They laughed again. "How do you feel?"

"My pussy is throbbing. I wish you were inside of me."

"Don't worry, I'll be home soon." Robert said, licking his lips.

Carlton exited his car and walked casually up the side walk. No one was out. He moved around the side of the house undetected and found the bedroom window. She was in her panties and bra. He saw her pick up the cordless phone and leave out the room. He waited to see if she would return. After five minutes, he moved around to the back of the house and found her through the open bathroom window. She had taken her bra and panties off. She was in the tub and on the phone. He watched her carry on with her conversation and it aroused him more by the second. He wanted to have her, possess her, take her. Flashes of taking her blinded him. He slams her soaking wet body onto the bed. She tries to scramble away but he grabs her by the ankles and pulls her closer. With considerable speed, she reaches up and punches him in face. It sounds off with a loud connection. He grabs her by the throat and pushes her back down onto the bed. He maintains control, choking her while he forces himself between her legs. He looks down on her with an evil, fixated look. It was just a vision. He snaps out of it.

She is still on the phone.

Robert says into the phone, "Touch it for me Baby."

Dayna put two fingers into her pussy. She pulled them out then rubbed around the lips, then goes back in deep. She swiveled her hips on her fingers. Her middle finger searched for her G-spot. She found it and felt herself about to explode.

Carlton could see her playing with her pussy. His dick got so hard he could hardly stay focused.

Robert said, "You going to cum for me?"

"Oh yes Daddy. I'm about to cum."

A couple of strokes later Dayna was screaming into the phone that she was cumming and she was cumming hard.

The sounds had Carlton so hard he was ready to jump through the window and handle his bizness. Only he didn't want whoever she was talking to, to hear her being attacked but as soon as she got off the phone, it was on. She continued to talk on the phone for a while then suddenly she got out of the tub still with the phone to her ear. She wrapped a towel around herself and headed to the living room for her glass of wine. Carlton climbed through the window quietly. The candles provided the air with the smell of jasmine. He didn't know where she was but he could hear her voice. He played out in his mind, what he is going to do to her. When he saw her he was going to run up behind her, put her in a choke hold position and over power her. He would bend her over and ram his cock into her vagina from the back, dry walls or not. She would try to fight against him and break free of his grip on her but to no avail and breaking a few nails in the process. She would be locked in his clutch. She would feel the coarseness of his clothes on her skin. He would continue to pound her relentlessly until his cum was flowing down her legs. He would drag her to a closet and continue to doggyfuck her inside of it with the door closed.

She would regret ever treating him as if he was unworthy and he bets she won't treat anyone that way again. He had not seen her since he had broken in, but he heard her voice moving around the house. He stealthily stepped into the hallway. Her voice was right around the bend, coming in his direction.

"Oh Robert, I am so glad you won the competition, I knew you would. So is it over, will you be coming home soon. I can't wait to see you. No don't get off the phone, talk to me a little while longer, I'll play with myself and cum for you again, Robert."

"Okay, if you insist Dayna."

"Okay, I'm gonna get in the bed so I can really get it for you."

She stopped short and turned around, heading into the bedroom. Carlton had stepped into the tub and was hiding behind the

301

shower curtain. He waited until she was laying on her back with her legs parted. Carlton peeked into the room.

Dayna had her index and middle fingers in her mouth, lubricating them for what she was about to do. She sunk the middle finger into her hot box and moaned seductively. This excited Robert through the phone. Carlton's dick screamed for her. Dayna moaned again as her eyes and head went back. Her feet pointed towards the sky, shook a little then separated from each other into a split. The whole time she was rubbing her clit, messaging it in a rapid circular motion. She put her feet flat on the bed and raised her hips in grand satisfaction.

"Oooh yeah Robert! Can I put my finger inside?"

"Yeah, put two fingers in there Vickie."

"Oooh, I touched my G-spot! Can I touch it again Daddy?"

"Yes Baby, but don't just touch it, stay on it for a while."

Carlton's dick was busting cum all down his leg, inside of his pants. The situation was too arousing. She had just advertised what he had fantasized about for five years. His dick was still jumping in small spasms and pumping out cum. He could wait no longer. He stepped into the hallway. Suddenly, Carlton heard a sound coming from the front room. It was the front door. He heard a voice say, "Where are you right now?"

Carlton heard Dayna say, "I'm still on the bed on my back with my legs open."

Carlton backed into the bathroom. Robert undressed in the living room, put the phone down and snuck into the bedroom.

Carlton peeked from behind the shower curtain and saw Robert's defined muscular frame as he passed. Robert stood over Dayna. She had the phone to her ear. Her eyes were closed and her legs were open. He dove on top of her, grabbed her head from both sides and pressed his lips hard against hers. She fought frantically from fright. She lifted a leg to kick but instead got a dick quickly rammed up in her soaking wet vagina. Once Robert pumped his stiff cock in and out of Dayna's pussy four or five times she quickly realized who it was. She stopped fighting, relaxed and let him beat the pussy up. He would dig deep twenty or thirty times then pull out. He would slide it back through her slippery opening and dig deep again. He would pull out then pump the head of his dick in and out the opening thirty or forty times. This would drive her crazy!

Then he would go deep for forty or fifty more strokes.

Carlton could hear Dayna scream that she was cumming as he made his way back out of the bathroom window.

Dayna busted a fat nut and dropped off to sleep in Robert's arms.

Carlton wanted no trouble with Robert. He left, never to return.

About two months passed, Carlton was sitting at home watching the news when a local car accident appeared on the screen. The picture caught his attention. It kinda looked like the guy Carlton saw creeping into Dayna's house that night he had almost got his revenge on her. Then the name Robert Cameron came on the screen. Carlton had heard her say Robert on the phone. It was his him, he was dead. Hmmm. he thought, Then Dayna was in front of the camera crying. Carlton's dick got hard as soon as he saw Dayna. She turned him on, even in her weakened condition.

Carlton felt like he had just been invited over by the girl of his dreams. For the first time in his life, Carlton felt like luck was on his side. After all of my suffering, he thought. Guess who's...

HOPE YOU ENJOYED THE RIDE!
Biz-e-Bee Book Group